a woman's influence

◆

a woman's influence

◆

johnny robert durham III

Writers Club Press
San Jose New York Lincoln Shanghai

a woman's influence

Writers Club Press
an imprint of iUniverse, Inc.

For information address:
iUniverse, Inc.
5220 S. 16th St., Suite 200
Lincoln, NE 68512
www.iuniverse.com

Any resemblance to actual people and events is purely coincidental.
This is a work of fiction.

ISBN: 0-595-22687-6

Printed in the United States of America

I never knew the man. I never knew my first words would be of Him. His legacy has survived these years to become something of myth and majesty. Growing up, listening to people talk about Him and what He meant to so many. Well, it made me uncomfortable. For two reasons. One, how do you live up to the gene pool expectation. And two…well it gets really boring. I mean I assume its bad enough having to hear story after story about your own family, from your family. But…to hear people constantly saying either clever words or invented drama to psycho analyze Him, and us, is a bit disturbing.

I have come to realize, having to grow up in this shadow that there is no room for mistake. Having camera crews permanently parked on the outskirts of your vision, as you try to contemplate life through a window. It all comes back. And yes it does disturb me. But my point is, or maybe it's the wisdom in growing up in what many would call a dream life style.

Is.......to get away from his shadow, I must delve into it. There have been many books written about my Grandfathers' Life. This will be the first from a Family member, as you all know. They said Grandfather would do his best at keeping us away from such things, as the press. That was one of those baffling things about Him. He loved His job. He hated the attention. That was a hard time with Grandmother though. As she was a natural cameras' flash. A starlit. In a psychology class once our assignment was to think of our earliest thought. And analyze it. I often wondered if the teacher didn't ask us to do this more for my recollection. In any case it was of Grandmother. I don't know if it was real or a dream, to this day. I remember being held by someone, so I must have been young. And I saw sadness in her eyes and in a face that tried to hold composure. And then she looked at me and smiled, I made her smile when she was sad. There was flashing in the sky. And maybe even loud music. And that's all I remember. As you all know, Grandmother is in seclusion. When Father took over the Empire, he hired a topnotch staff and built her a mansion. Some say its for the Rich nut, I still find that remark less than appealing. And it's not because She has Her blood in me. It's just sad. These people, who so loved my Grandfather, still say such hypocritical garbage.

So I delve into the past, with this Family tree the world has wanted to read since my Grandfather's death. I haven't seen my Grandmother, well since that earliest memory of my childhood, again if that's what it was. She stays in her room at the Nuthouse. I hear that her days are filled with talking to The Dead. Remembering things long forgotten. Longing for her chance to hear the sweet words of Grandfather, whispered in her ear. You may ask. Why haven't I seen her in all this time? I guess it's because of the mansion. Father took me one time to see her. Him and Mother. I was so scared. I was four or five then. And I screamed and ran out the door. That's what I was told any-way. A young child smelling the misery and heartache. And I still wonder to this day, why. It was clean, father loved her. Most especially Grandmother, its a magical home. A place I hate myself for not playing in as a child. So tomorrow I make my journey away from college. Hugs and kisses to the folks, and I will visit my Grandmother for, I guess the first time. I can barely contain the self-loathing of not getting to see her and talk about him sooner. So the antici-pation is great, but the fear is worse. I will try to unlock the mystery, that has been self-imposed by the Media. I will get to know my Grandmother. I will get to know about the man most everyone called President. I will get to know the man I once called Paw-Paw.

The Big Day

The morning snow on the ground outside of my lonely apartment window, signified the end of another turn of my life, a partial-life crisis; my sub-conscience would say. I went over in my head, 'had I packed everything?' And other meaningless jargon. The worry of things totally obliviously worthless blotted out by a comforting fit of O.C.D. But no matter how I denied the thought of another woman in the back of my mind, with spells of knowing forgetfulness. She wouldn't go away. And without warning the snow I once saw contained Julie and I. Having a conversation we have had over an over. As the snow wiped itself in her hair and against her jeans and leather jacket. "What's wrong with you," she blurted? "Why do you want to change me so much," I questioned? "This last year of college HAS changed you! Remember how we had fun. Those carefree days? Those endless intoxicated nights?" Again her words had a sharp crispness that lately has stung. Her body contorted with a look of disappointment as she continued. "Are we growing apart? Are we becoming your worst fear..........A MARRIED COUPLE?" Her eyes went wet and in between sobs. "The boring bathroom love, is that all we are? Say something!" I was there. Not all of me, just that me that couldn't think of the right thing to say. A first date gone south. A love affair, and she was asking me for closure, a divorce in some sense. I opened my mouth to speak but nothing more came out. And as I so didn't want her to go. She turned, like some little child, disappointed, and walked into the snow, away from me, and out of the picture. Just like that day long ago and last night. As my trance quickly left and I stood at the window. Still no thought of what I should have said and how I should have phrased it took hold. Just those lines, 'why do you want to change me?' Why did she want the old me back? And what was that old, younger version? All I know of me now, is a constant wonder of what it was like to be me yesterday. Every morning when I wake up, the same question. What now? The stage in life when deprogram an analyze takes hold the strongest; and for that brief eternity, nothingness/blankness is given to you in the form of the earliest childhood questions.

The Car

The limo ride home was as usual. Several Ferrari bodyguards keeping the Princess killing vultures with un-human x-ray lenses, at bay from the stretched chariot. A drink and the soft melodies of the darkness played against the backdrop of my mind. Or in other words, Jack Daniels and Sugar Rays,' SOMEDAY,' lightly playing in the background. The ride home left a void, which was consumed by Julie. Aloud I vocalized my memory's, to the micro-cassette recorder.

How Julie and I met!

Father, being the generous man that he has always been. And knowing I have a penchant for loneliness, bought me an apartment off campus, fully furnished with necessities and a ROOM-MATE. His name was Ron. He was born endowed, not as much me, however. This Ron was a Senior, my inaugural year. He was like a cool glass of Vodka and a warm shot of piss. Shaken not stirred or dribbled. He was the poster boy for anal retentiveness, though he partied, hard. The chit-chat aside, of getting to know one another. He turned out to be the Headman on campus. And that night, before classes were to start, we went to what he described as a drunken orgy, or at least it had the possibilities. The first thoughts in my head were.

'This is college, but I am not into experimentation with the same sex.' The Secret Service only stared at each other, their one time solemn faces now showed the concern of parents with no say so.

Arriving and entering the Fraternity House was a nightmare. Drunks and loud mouths consumed the air inside and outdoors. A pleasant surprise was in the time that past. No one seemed to know me or at least they did a good job of acting the part. It was actually more like curious glances disguised as non-interest. The crowd was quite obsessed with Ron, as well. And the chit chat aside, I didn't care for Ron. When I walked in the door of the frat house, he bumped me out of the way. And that I did not forgive!

Being the way that I am, like I've said, I kept to myself. Ron didn't introduce me. He just assumed, something, I don't know what. His body language emphasized, do your own thing, I can't baby-sit you. You should be so honored as the person that walked in with me! Yes, that was what it was, that bastard, in my boiling new-found hatred a voice, came. "Hi. I know you," she said with a drunken sway and cute know-it-all pout. "Your Johnny Robert Durham the firsts, grandson, so I guess that makes you the Third. He meant more to this Country than anyone could ever dare to repay. I'm sorry you must get this attention all the time," she said as she looked around, only to late for the mass heads moved away from us in unity. "Well, I guess I'll see you around," she said as she turned. "Wait," and in that moment. I had made a very spontaneous decision. Talking. Talking to her. But what would I say as she slowly turned. Closer to an answer to that question, she crept. "I was just wondering would you like to have a drink sometime?" Her smile said it all, in bright, upward contortions. "Yes," she said holding her meaningful smile and she turned again. "Wait," and she turned again, the smile somewhat faded. "Yes." "Can right now be sometime? I ask because," I paused and looked down, starting to feel foolish. And then it hit me. A perfect line. "What I mean by right now is......we never know if we'll have the time." All right it wasn't great, but progress. She smiled with that sharp feminine coyness, of GOTTCHA.

Our walk back to her place

After a couple shots of Vodka an awkward small talk, on my part, I asked if I could walk her home and she agreed. The warm summer breeze that night took on a chill of an approaching fall. Her hair was much shorter then, but the wind still made it wave to and fro. And the only thoughts in my head were of truly corny lines, that she would only figure to be bedroom estimations, if I dare spoke them. "Why don't you talk? I mean, you come from a great oracle family." My face gave a involuntary look of disgust. And as I looked at her I knew she felt she had hurt me, and blameless as I could plea. I hurt her too. "I am so sorry. You must get that type of comment all the time. I bet it's hard to be yourself, let alone get a feeling of whom you are. And I am somewhat to blame. I guess its like meeting someone you have always wanted to meet. In a way. Not that you're not someone I would not want to know. Damn-it.......I'm not using you. I would just like to get to know you. And I don't want to sleep with you," her face was away from me and she didn't see my look of DAMN! At that last comment. Then she turned and continued, "I didn't mean it like that! OH! GOD, you must think I am some type of dumb bimbo, groupie. Don't you?" She turned even closer to me with wide doe eyes. Sure I knew what she was talking about. I guess to a point, the thing is I have met all the people I admire. And now they are friends. And that sucks because I get ragged about the gushing I once gave. Her eyes were so beautiful. Like deep, blue rivers; with bass in them. "You want to know why I don't talk?" Her face was steady and glued to mine, waiting for the mysterious veil to be lifted. "I don't like putting my foot in my mouth and having to explain what my true meaning is. Kind of like what you just did" I smiled and her face went from shock to 'you asshole,' with a smirk on top. And then it was like every guys nightmare. The perfect setting with the perfect girl. And a shit head comes along and totally takes your dignity. Ron, that bleeping bleep!

Ron and his soon to be unfortunates

It was like in slow motion. I knew something bad was about to go down. The looks on the four of their faces, as the car slowed nearing us. I caught a brief glance of Julie's face and it too showed signs of worry. And then Ron opened his loud mouth. "Hey BOY, you were supposed to wait for me. I never gave you permission to leave." His smirk told the never-ending story. The primitive primate that has to show up the guy with the cute chick. In hopes that she'll say something along the lines of, 'yeah baby. I love a smart-ass man, who belittles other's pride: in a vain attempt to sleep with the cute chick. And oh, you know those type of guys are the ones you want to spend the rest of your lives with.' I grimaced somewhat. Wishing this was a nightmare. But he wouldn't let it go. "Hey BOY. I'm talking to you. Who's your pretty little honey? I heard about you, Julie. Is it true you got drunk and let twenty guys do whatever they wanted?" His gaze, now with a look of animal hate; as his buffoon's giggled a drunken laugh, now shifted back to me. "Get in the car, NOW, BOY!" I turned back to Julie, who's face, with tears falling like rivers, told me I had to do something. Father's words came back to haunt me. 'Always keep at least two body-guards with you at all times, SON!' I braced myself and turned back to them, only to hear Ron say, "I was just kidding, see you at home sweetheart." He laughed and the car sped off. I turned back to Julie. But what could I say. We were by her Sorority house, which was somewhat bitterly ironic. She tried to open her mouth, but she just turned and ran into the house. I called after her, "JULi," but the word trailed off.

The long walk home

It was like being in a fog or a deep shock. Why hadn't Father screened this guy, Ron, better? Or those eager to please Bastards that work for him. I replayed the last few moments in my head. What should I have said? What would Grandfather have done? See that was a critical phase of my wonderment of Grandfather. He was the one no one messed with. The one they all feared. And then I realized, the question was the answer. He would never let those pests get away with such a thing. Though I dare say, they wouldn't have had the balls to do it in the first place. I remembered once how he beat a man to death, when my Father was an infant, an almost run over, by some fellow. The guy, with cell-phone still in hand, actually had the Gaul to get out of the car and bitch at Grandfather. He must have been living under a rock for quite some time, for he had no idea of whom he was dealing with. A mass surrounded to watch the dire event that was about to unfold. Grandfather walked over to the man. And beat him to death! Well that's the story. And he did it in a cool sane manor. It is still to this day an unsolved mystery. It seems, out of all of those people that were gathered, none could remember what happened. And wouldn't you know it. The man had no family and was thoroughly disliked. I heard his neighborhood actually had a parade in honor of his leaving of this mortal time.

And out of my trance I came. Looking at MY apartment, with that haunting car in the drive. And those loud, poor souls in MY apartment. Not knowing how they had helped me, in humiliation, strive to discover my roots. At that moment I was the most dangerous man alive, and all I had was a cell-phone.

Our first date

It didn't take long for several cars to arrive to my beckoning. Ten black Lincolns and one stretched limo, for me. The men calmly got out of the car and walked up to me, two being the Secret Service guys I have mentioned before. I was astounded by their size and number. They all had to be some type of professional body-builders. Forty-five in all followed me up the steps. I turned and smiled at their blank faces and said, "just wait out here." I slowly turned the doorknob, figuring it would be unlocked. They didn't notice me right off, these victims inside. But when the door closed a little to hard they all turned to me. They weren't faces of evil. They weren't faces of owners of my dignity. And for a split second I questioned my judgment, until, "Go get us a drink," Ron laughingly barked. And that face came back, that face that I still have ingrained in my head. A smirk, a bitch slap of contempt. But I stood there. His face went more stern now. And his seating situation took a leap forward. As he halfway leaned out of the chair. And his friends followed. But then he smiled. "Look, John, you don't want to piss me off. See I like you, sort of. And people around here respect me. Now I know your family is some big shit, but it doesn't scare me. My families not so weak ourselves. But that's not the point. The point is, John, I don't get scared." His face was of a loving parent, teaching what's right and wrong. And his tone and manner, were that of a Micheal Corelone. And how dare he! "Now I'll say again, John, go get us our drinks. And while your at it John, Honey, order a pizza." I slowly turned around and turned the doorknob. And our walls were filled with a never ending engulfing swarm of black suits. Ron, was almost left of his good friends. But when each tried to get up they found a gun barrel blocking their path. I calmly sat. Wiped off my sweaty palms on my pants and stared at Ron, with a look of distain. "Why did you say, Julie slept with twenty men? Or what was it?" My question only made Ron gulp. I blew out a breath and looked down. "Ron," I looked up again, "your going to be punished in many, many, many ways. But no matter what the truth is, Ron. Your going to be punished more. You and your friends. If what you say is not the truth. Now I know you might think the truth is only going to hurt me, Ron. If it is the case that something happened, Ron. And I dare say something did, Ron! Honey. Because only a guy with no sense of compassion at all, would say a thing to a young lady, for no just reason." His eyes only grew in size. I stood up and this time they leaned back. I paced back and forth. Sometimes being hid by the massive masses. I was a shadow, but always there. Coming in an out of the light. My steps were soft but imposing on the hardwood floor and on the ear. "I want all of you to focus on your most intimate body parts.' Think how comfortable they are. But if I don't get some answers, real soon."

The Limo ride to Julie's

The drive was calming and a bit comical. Though I did not laugh at these fresh and blood. I had found out the reason of Ron's comments. Julie was applying for a Sorority. And to get in she had to prove herself. The test was go to a neighboring Fraternity and in her pledge, sexually gratify three guys. She went so far as going in, but her virtue held true. And she past the test. Because if she 'did' these guys, she would not only not get in. She would be left with the labeled humiliation of a whore. **So she was accepted, though her Sisters forgave her. In her innocent naive character, she later found out she was the only one to have gone that far. And she was forever, on that campus; discriminated, as within reach of being easy. Her resilience prevailed. And respect came, from the majority.**

The long lines of cars stopped and I, accompanied by a few of my men, got out and made

our way to the door. My resolve weakened as I
just realized how late it was. But the rooms were
all lit. I rang the bell and within seconds a to
fresh freshman with big black glasses, messed up
teeth and pig tails answered. I felt an arousal
brewing below the belt. She was most certainly
untouched. Probably wouldn't have been that
hard to get to touch her. But her face hardened,
and a brutal militant dike emerged, with a loud;
and angry voice. "Do you know how late it is?
Do you want me to call security? Tonight no
man shall enter. For I am the keeper of the night,
it is my pledge and so shall it be!" "What the hell
are you talking about," I asked, with a laugh?
"Look just get Julie, she never said her last
name." And I described her. But again that idi-
otic yelling, statement. I guessed it could only be
some pre-anti-rape measure, outside of the stu-
pid local demand. I had just about had enough.
No little loud mouth female, or anyone for that
matter was going to stop my mission, tonight.
What would I say to those naked guys in the car.
This little runt was ruining my big surprise. I
leaned in close and yelled. "Get Julie, you dumb
bitch! I am not going to hurt her. She'll forgive
you!" The moment my lips and body pulled
from her ear. I felt bad. She was still hanging on
strong, but tears were in her mad eyes. As she

looked down, I saw fear. "What's going on," her familiar voice sent my little heart to pattering. "Julie," I said as I saw her body define itself from the depths of the inside darkness. "Johnny, is that you? What are you doing here? Do you know what time it is?" Her right hand came up and laid itself on the one I'll call, Innocence' shoulder. Julie's face turned and looked at her tearful eyes. Her face shot me a glance of pure hatred. Bulging eyes, bared, clinching teeth. "I am sorry. I just had to see you." "I don't want to see any man tonight. You should have been smart enough to figure that out." Her voice was raw and almost terrifying. She began to pull Innocence inside. "Wait, that's why I came, haven't you ever done anything totally at the wrong time and it was so meaningful to the other person, in your eyes, that you couldn't not let them see it? You can go inside. You can think I am some kind of freak. But there's something in that Limo that will make up for what those jerks said to you!" Again, this is some kind of chick, I thought. I was never so bold before. Her face scanned the men with me. "They are just some bodyguards. We're not gang-rapists." She pushed Innocence back inside and stepped out. She looked at me with child like curiosity. Her gown was baby blue and went down to her shins.' Though I would have preferred panties only. This, though, had a pleasant delightful sexualness to it, that made me feel comfortable. "So, are you just going to look at me or show me what's so damn great that's going to make up for what those mother————- said?" If I ever cared or wondered, if what I was about to show her would freak her out, it subsided right there. I took her hand and gently lead her to the Limo, as my loyal men stood firm, just a few steps behind.

The big Laugh

I opened the door and she made her way inside gracefully. I saw her face was in a shock, but amused. And when I sat beside her, she started to laugh. Yes these four were quite comical. Naked, tiny penis' unconcealed. Sweat pouring. Gag's in their mouths.' Fear and humiliation in the Limo! I handed her a dozen roses, I had picked up on the way. And arranged my self on the opposite side of the car. It was just the six of us. I sat with my back to the driver. She sat with her back at the trunk. And they sat with their backs to the left side windows. We talked and laughed about trivial things. Our first date was everything, and more I could have ever dreamed of. After hours of meaningful and meaningless dribble. We arrived at our destination. The car slowed and Ron and his unlucky fellows, showed an inevitable look of more fear. "Why did we stop?" I let Julie's question loom around. I turned and watched the four's eyes, look every which way. What could be going through their minds I thought? Then I turned back to her. "Lets get out." And with that, the doors opened. Julie made her way out. A few of my associates grabbed whatever convenient body part of the purp's, and drug; an I followed. Outside of the car, all eyes were on me. One Bodyguard asked something like, "what do you want us to do? Beat them? We have that gay guy that you asked for." I heard Ron and his Cronies start to whimper. And then they struggled, until fists started controlling them. I turned my gaze to Julie. "It's up to her. What do you want." My mind was in diabolical overdrive. "We can beat them to death. Or just beat them. The gay guy can you know. Whatever you want for your peaceful sleep!" Her laugh was genuine. Her face was tender. But her heart was of gold. "Just let them go. The waiting and wondering is the worse part." I breathed out a long, "SHUUUUUU." And turned to Ron, with occasional glances at his gomba's. "Well. I guess your ass is safe. But I hope you learned a lesson." And I stepped forward, eye to eye with the enemy, Ron. "I can have you killed. Sodomized and videotaped. I can tell the world this and use our real name's. And I can get away with it. I am your GOD. And you reside in the palm of my hand." His large eyes, scanned my held up palm. That quickly clinched tight. From there this fist of fury. I simply put the other hand to it, and wiped back and forth, to clean itself of the symbolic dirt.

They were promptly put in one of the awaiting cars. And driven back to their, soon to be, former residences.' Ron quickly retrieved his belongings. Most he left. In, what I guess, a fear to not take something his warped mind might think was rightfully mine now. I later heard that he moved out of the Country and changed his name. As well as his friends. We stood there for awhile, Julie an I. Staring at each other with a smirk. A puppy dog love. A newfound relationship born of a tragedy. Born from two legacy's that combined perfectly.

Back to my ride Home

The Driver pulled over at a rest stop, to do his nature functions. I myself worried about the homosexual overtones, at such a place. Out the window I looked. A man and woman, in a bitter argument. Again memories clouded the view, and paralleled to the idea's I had just recently embarked on.

With what I did to Ron, and the raving couple; wanting to hurt each other. I thought again about the theory of getting even. And of course I remembered a story I was told about Grandfather. One I am certain, you have not heard, dear audience. It involved his love hate relationship with humans; as he called them. It all started months after he graduated from college. He went out of town with an old friend, Jake, to a party his brother was throwing. I don't remember his brothers' name. Anyway. As it turned out. This friend of Grandfathers,' ex-girlfriend- who I'll call Melissa The dike- was there. And for reasons I don't know they disliked each other. Through most of the party they kept there distance, an ensured this with not so friendly looks. But every time Grandfather's gaze accidentally swept past her and her clique. One of this Melissa's friends' eyed him. Later that night. When the crowd started to die down. Grandfather and Jake strolled down the hall, in way of the kitchen, to retrieve drinks from the refrigerator. I can't remember exactly how it went. But I think it was something like this. "What do you mean you think he's cute. He's an asshole. He's crazy. I hate him. Why would you want to be around someone that your friend hates?" Melissa's back was turned from the hall that led to the kitchen. When her friends' eyes widened. She knew, she knew. Grandfather walked in slowly. Jake looked down with shame, and worry at what the future held. Melissa turned, hauntingly. They say Grandfather's eyes were extremely dark and menacing. And then he spoke. "If you have any idea of how much I hate you. You'd be scared stiff, standing this close. If you knew how much I hate you this moment, the goodness in you would weep. If you ever say anything about me again, even if it's a comple-ment, I will pray every night to any Deity that will listen; at 9:00 pm eastern standard time. That you die a painful death." The last anyone said about what happened to this girl was that she joined a convent, how funny those life's ironies. Moral of the story, it takes a little hate and bickering, to commune with the humanity; we sorely lack. Unfortunately, it seldom works that way. And we usually just hate more harder. Wow! That's deep.

There were more pleasantries, though

Grandfather was a man most wanted to be like. Not because of money, or looks, power, or family heritage. It was spiritual. Now knowing about him, in a sense of- The ones we are influenced to be influenced by. Yes the majority do think he was great. After hearing that bit of family secrecy, and the alleged fact that he once beat a man to death. You may say. Are you trying to say, by delving in to his past. Your telling us he was bad. No, that's non-sense. How dare you. He had his good days. It's rumored he once was watching the Nightly News. And, of course, it had to do with the Jews and Palestinians. Or Palestinians and Jews, if that's more politically correct. Now where was I, Oh! yes. This man and his young son. The son couldn't have been more than eight. They were caught in a crossfire. The father shielded his son. But the bullets, in the end, prevailed. The world was aghast, for a long few days when that bit of reality television hit brainwaves. And Grandfather, amongst his friends, cried. He often wept for strangers. A true sign of a person this world should be made up by. He commented on that some years later. As you may well remember. When asked one thing he wished he could have done, in an interview. He exclaimed, "I wish I could have walked toward them in that horrific gunfire. Not for ego's sake of course. But maybe that would have stopped those bullets. Imagine a place so holy consumed by fear. And an American at that, saving those Palestinians. Even if I died there. I think something greater could have been accomplished, more than anything I have or will ever do. His truthfulness started a chain reaction.

Less hate, even now; a radical concept. Maybe we just have to pick our battles. Maybe we can pay it forward. Maybe this world isn't a lost cause.

Finally at Home

The limo pulled into the drive and my stomach knotted at the well wishers.

The gathering was allot smaller than I first imagined. Old friends who work for my father. The dwindling staff that attends to grandmother. As well as many relatives I don't know, and, or course, father beaming proudly next to mother. The car slowed. And with each phase of the curb approaching closer. The reaction of getting out made my stomach churn. Once out of the car, everyone smiled and shook my hand. Asked how I was, and offered advice. Mothers' lipstick blurred my cheeks. Fathers' hand dragged me off. We made no small talk on the way to his office. Inside the interrogation began over my favorite drink. "So still like the same drink? How does it go again?" father asked with a air of glad nostalgia. "Glass, ice, Jack, cherry-coke, a small dollop of whip-cream on top, and a little red straw to mix contents." We sat awhile. Not knowing what to say. Or how to say something that would not end with arguing. "So how's the Middle east ," I began? "Oh! Just constant bitching back and forth. They're like little children the both of them. It still sickens me that on such a holy land, hate, is the mentor of everyone. Still calling me the second Anti-Christ. They must think I am plotting something by living between them. How dare he keep us peaceful," he yelled; as, he turned to the victim window, of the world. But enough about me. We're here to celebrate you. We are so proud of you. I hate to sound cliche,' but any plans?" I was somber and a bit to sober to know exactly what to say. If I told the truth, that I was aiming to write about Grandfather, father would win. Winning I mean the age old lesson he has tried to teach. I still hear it in my head, 'one day you'll want to know your heritage.' Since he will find out anyway, I thought at the time, why not be honest. "I want to write a book about Grandfather." He looked odd. But just raised his eyebrows and downed his last swallow. "Whom will you be interviewing," he asked? The question made me rethink this plot. I hadn't thought of whom I would talk with, outside the immediate family. The puzzled look on my face said to him that the very simple idea had not even crossed my mind. He walked over to a video-cassette cabinet and retrieved a cassette. "Here watch this. Sometimes its best to start at the end, as you make your way toward it."

I pocketed the video and made my way back to well wishers. And after talking to everyone twice, I made my way to my bedroom of years past. I scanned through old memorabilia of the room I spent so many years of solitary in, and plopped down on my cozy bed; micro-cassette recorder out, to watch the video. The quality was magnificent. Sound bites from celebrity Newspersons. Ted Koppell referring to the media leaving our family alone for once by saying, 'the day the paparazzi......went away.' I bet people are envious of such a well choreographed funeral. Standing room only, as thousands of people inside watched proceedings. Media Mogul's, President's, Actor's, Foreign Dignitary's, and countless others were on the prestigious guest list. Thousand's more were outside and billions more watched, Grandfather's last television extravaganza. Many people longing for a chance to get up to the podium and tell what He meant to so many. And finally Father, the last to give testimony and final grievance in a never ending eulogy. His approach to the loneliest place in the world, the pulpit, was showmanship. Calm, cool, hard faced; but, humble. Hard to imagine such a feat. At the podium the microphone collected his throat clearing. The camera's caught his youthful glow. And the world got its first glimpse of the son of a Philanthropist. "I....................." and he broke down. And like the father figure he had always been. President George W. Bush stepped up and took over. With his familiar pat on the back and a mouth moving smile that invoked words of wisdom, in Father's ear. Father with a smile but with grief stricken tears went to his seat. The former President cleared his throat and turned on an oratory charm that Hitler would have envied. "I......and with tears that followed. That is profound. It says it all. We are a nation hurt. And after all we have been through our soul is still weak, but yet so strong. We are a powerful contradiction. It's hard when anyone dies. President Durham would say. But I think when someone who has done so much dies, it hurts a little more. Where can I start? Maybe He came into my life after the retribution bombing started for the September 11 tragedy. In his emails I found wisdom. A fresh breath to evil. When he got on Islamic chat rooms and said stop. 'STOPPPPP.........hating these people for skin color. For a religion that was manipulated. Because if we hate these people, my fellow humans, we let the terrorists win. We will not be the Country we once strived to be. A nation of all nationalities. A nation not using our brains.' I am paraphrasing, but that was his dream. Imagine a

Country that takes the hate and gives love. And we did, with a tad attrition. When he said those words, 'the lost art of pen pal diplomacy,' and, 'a child shall lead them.' He reminded me in those emails. This could be an awakening of clever spirituality. And so I speak words unscripted and not very well worded. In a tribute to a hero. A hero we try to aspire to. A hero of immense value and of values. A hero that will be missed and martyred."

As I watched this great President, I was reminded of what Grandfather was. They said Grandfather loved President Bush. He was once quoted as saying, 'I always wanted to smoke a joint with President Clinton, but I would have loved to drink a beer with Presy Georgie.' When the funeral ended. I was surprised by the collected collage of memories I never knew. Memories surrounding those terrible events of September 11. Those sights shown with a Forrest Gump soundtrack of past lives. With patriotic flag faces, people marched in the street. With open check books, the popular mafia slogan; we take care of our own, became something that defined a generation. And with pure defiance, those who wanted to hurt us and make us run in terror. Only infuriated and brought about anger. And with painted signs in the streets, thanking the firepersons and police. A Country forged a new spirit. And with those immortal words, 'we will not go gently into that goodnight. We will not vanish without a fight.' We won, we showed those who wanted to intimidate that we would not stand for there of. And with actions, we did overcome. We looked fear in the face and showed what true fear can be. And midst we gave love. With food falling from the air to peasants who suffered. We took care of people that terrorists had little care for, except to pollute with hate filled corruption. Our new Bob Hope inspiration came in the form of Hollywood idols. And our great leader Bush. Hugging a fireman on top of rubble. Giving a pep talk to a city that so vehemently once discouraged him. Well it was history. Our flag would never go down. And with tears in his eyes he comforted families, like he did for my father. And his wife was equally impressive. Her mothering soft quality, her fabulous frame accented in red gowns, her smile that held hearts in her mind. These two made Grandfather, and defined a Nation. It was only fitting that President Bush gave the eulogy.

I relaxed from my weary mind wonder. I laid back on the bed, exhausted, defeated. Wondering what mystery's will be unlocked when I awaken tomorrow and meet Grandmother. Will she have that First Lady charm and Actress wit, she was so known for. Or will she be a stranger who knows nothing of my guilt? Sleep. Sleep. Sleep.

The next Morning

The day started off like no other. I was in a daze. Half aware that sometime today questions would be answered. Locked lies undone. I was a zombie at breakfast. Only giving grunts. My parents gazed past the newspapers long enough to ask meaningless questions. But they understood, and prodding was neglected. I showered, longer than most. I put on my best suit. And finally came to my senses. Would I tell her who I was? If I did, would that hold the key to things unknown. If she asked why, after all this time, I wanted to know. Would that truth hold back her truth? Would I lie and hurt her, to spare her? Finally I finished with questioning, before I burnt myself out. Finally holding back the inevitable. Checking my appearance. GOD I felt like a chick saying she would take her blouse off but hesitating, hoping silently for an earthquake. I turned from the mirror. Took a deep breath and was on my way. Oh! shit, forgot the cassette recorder. Anything else? NO! Just go!

GRANDMOTHERS LAST STAND

◆

I stood before the massive arena like mansion. With its creepy old world castle style. The air had taken on a wind that was scary almost. I held back the laughter at the horror movie setting I conjured in my head. The path was clean, with renegade leaves to and fro. It felt like autumn here, this deeper south. As I made my way up the few steps and came upon the door, I stopped. I was her Grandson, should I not go in, straight away? I was a stranger should I knock? I did the latter. The door creaked slowly open. And a kindly faced older African lady smiled and ushered me inside. "Come on in. My have you grown." She said and shook her head. She knew me but I didn't know her. I wondered if she shook her head at how she must have aged or that she knew me only from diapers and infant rebellion? "I bet you haven't the slightest idea who I am know do you?" "No ma'am. But I guess you know me." I said with a smile. "Why

yes I know you," and she gave my arm a push.
"I've been taking care of your Grandmother
since before you were born. I was much younger
then. So..............Your Father told me the
reason of your visit. I also am aware of how awkward this must be. I wouldn't worry. She never
gets any visitor's. And I am sure she won't recognize you." With that she turned and began leading me to my destination. Those last words cut
deep. I didn't take a step, "excuse me." She
turned with a questioning glance. "Why did she
agree to see me, if she won't know who I am?"
"Your Father didn't tell you. OH dear. Maybe
you shouldn't see her until you speak to him." I
grimaced. "What do you mean," but she lingered. "Look Mrs......" And I glanced at her
badge. "Gloria. Mrs. Gloria, look I will find out
anyway. Nothing is wrong with her.........is
there?" She didn't speak for a few moments, the
floor held her gaze. Finally she looked me
strongly in the eye. "She's dying. Your father told
her, since she's been quiet all these years, she
should talk to a reporter one last time. He told
her she owed the world that much." Mrs.
Gloria's face smiled with the final remark, "Your
Dad said you are a great reporter." She turned
again and without words, only remorse, I followed. As we approached the door she turned

again and with a soft, almost whispering tone, said, "Your Grandmother doesn't leave these rooms. There are just three. Her bedroom, a bathroom, and what you will be entering, the private living room." She turned to knock on the door but I stopped her. "Is there anything I should know. I mean she doesn't leave right, so she must have some type of. I hate to say mental condition. I just don't want to do anything wrong." My eyes pleadingly employed. Her disappointed face, softened. "No honey child. She's quick, so you watch out. She's known for messin' with reporters." And she pointed a hard finger. Finally she turned to the door. "Ms. Durham….The reporters here." "Send him in," the voice that should have triggered a thousand memories didn't. I wiped the sweat forming on my brow and slowly turned the doorknob.

Peaking through the door came dull light. Which I soon learned was from the fireplace straight ahead. I patiently walked in and took a quick glance around. To the far left were bookshelves with a rigged hangar, that held a red evening gown. To the far right, more bookshelves and oddly enough a poster of Bob and Arnold. And just in the slight chance you have been living under a rock for many years. They were, and still are, considered the worlds leading

potheads. They also saved Grandfathers life
once. I'll be sure to ask Grandmother about that.
I turned my gaze back to the center again and
above on the mantel was a baseball. A red gown,
a poster; out of place, and a baseball. Strange, I
thought. "Come here, young one," I heard her
tender voice say. My GOD she sounded like a
vampire and I shuttered? It came from the direction of the fireplace. The poorly lit room glis-
tened on two chairs in front of the fire. And an
old withered hand glowed, perched on an arm-
rest. I stepped softly, as to not break the old,
creaky floor. Closer I came to her, and, and. I
peered over her chair to see a genuine smile.
"Have a seat. My your handsome for a reporter.
Reporter's were not so handsome when I was
your age." I sat down. Again the need arose to
wipe my forehead. "Where are you from, dear?"
"Well I grew up around here actually, but."
"No...I don't mean that. I mean who do you
write for?" "OH!.......I write for......a small
independent......movie   magazine.......The
Network Insider. Heard of it?" "Afraid not dear."
Great   my   first   conversation   with   my
Grandmother and I am already lying. Her face
showed age lines. Her auburn hair combed back.
Her old blue nightgown cascaded down and hid
her feet. "Can I ask you a question young man?"

"Sure." "Why you? Why now? What makes you so special that my son, who knows I hate the press……. Why you?" Her chin rested on her hand. And a devilish smile crossed her face as her body crept forward. "Well." Calmness hit me. I was my Grandfather's Grandson. I could bullshit with the best of them. And since I have already lied, why not continue? "I have always been a huge fan of this family. My father would talk endless about it. How important it was. There was a time I must confess that I became bored of it." A little lie with the truth always does do wonders. She pulled back with a satisfied grin. "There was a time when I was tired of it too. But with age, you have so little. Time takes away so much. And all you have is regret. Time you hope you can change if there is a heaven. For the hell you live is old age. You can see the world. But it still doesn't un-bottle the thoughts of family. Things that can't be taken back. Your young. I dare say you have many years ahead of you," her smile broke but my heart gave me hope from those words. "Would you like some advice from an old woman?" Her question lingered. It was as if she was speaking to the true me. Was she fucking with me, I wondered? "Sure," eventually came. "Don't wait. If you have people you have wronged. Make it right as soon as you can.

Or someday you may end up in an isolated room. Full of memories hanging on the wall," she gestured around at those that I have previously mentioned, "and regrets to much to bear." I cleared my throat and agreed. Her eyes twinkled in the glow of the fire. Her face lines gave way to blankness. "The only real regrets I have are of my husband. We had fight the day of his assassination." I sat still, waiting for her to go on, but nothing. "Well what do you want to talk about?" her impatience startled me back to life. "Why don't we talk about how you and your husband met. I know you have told it a million times. I ask because.............sometimes after the millionth time. We remember something new, forgotten. Remember the emotion. Or something." She stayed toneless. And to quickly she made a half turn, facing the left wall. "You see that red dress. I was wearing that. I wore it to his funeral, as well. And I bet I could still wear it and turn some heads," her face gave a sad little smile. "Well it all started one cool autumn day. I was well on my way to becoming the dynamite actress I always wanted to be. And I loved to travel. That particular day for some reason. Which I later found out was a set up. I was flying over a rocky canyon, somewhere in the heat and dirt of Arizona. The day was clear and the radio was playing Chris DeBurg's, "Lady in Red," which was dedicated to a gal with the same name as I. It was just me in back and my pilot, of course, in the front. We flew over this oddly shaped mountain." She turned to me. "Imagine a mountain that just goes straight up into the air. Not in a triangle form. But like a gigantic rectangle, setting on one of its edges. As we flew over I saw this man. And he was waving like he was in trouble." Her motions captured the many movies that have depicted this part. "Anyway he kept waving. I didn't know what to do. I mean I just couldn't leave him there. Should I tell my blind pilot to radio for help? So I pushed the call button and Jake, that was the pilots name, addressed me. I told him to make another pass over the mountain. So he did. I asked if there was enough room for him to land on it. He studied for a few moments. And we landed. This handsome man came running for the doors. At once I wondered if this was a mistake. I thought could it be one of those crazy reporters?" She smiled but made no gesture toward me. "Anyway , he hopped aboard. Finely dressed. That was another reason I was suspicious. For surely no man went rock climbing in a tuxedo. His smile was charming. He sat next to me and we started chatting. My first impression of this man, was not so good. He seemed to try to much. And contrary to popular belief, women hate that. I mean he was good looking but no Pierce Brosnan. 'What on earth were you doing on that peak.' Those were my first words. He smiled and said he was a novelist. Mind you nowhere on him were any writing utensils. So with a hard face I asked him about that. He smiled and turned his head. 'Well my dear what are you doing flying over such a mountain?' 'None of your business,' was my response. 'Fine,' he said, 'I could give a rat's asssssssssssss.' What nerve I thought. So I turned my head. And I said, 'if you must know, I am enjoying a pleasant view. Nothing more.' I thought that was quite enough. Then he blurted out the most rudest comment. 'Your quite the egotist. Do you always get this dressed up for a Sunday fly?' 'If you have to know, my clothes were damaged. Do you always get that dressed up for an evening on a mountain?' I rebuked! 'No. Its just something different to do. That's how I write and that's why I never get writers block. Just a theory.' He came in closer to me and continued. 'I don't think set- ting in front of the same computer with same old surroundings all day is good for a writer.' I gave him a look of less than caring. We flew in silence for some time and he after a while he

pulled out a pen and a small notebook, and
began writing. He seemed to enjoy it, he laughed
as he wrote. I was intrigued. This man said none
of the usual garbage. He didn't try and flatter
me. I knew something had to be up. 'What are
you writing?' I demanded. 'Nothing about you.
That's what your thinking isn't it, that I must be
some sleezy reporter trying to get the dirt on
why your flying.' His remark was to sarcastic.
But since we would be spending a few hours
together on our way back. I tried to sound
somewhat interested. So I faked looking hurt."
She turned to me and said, "that's a secret
women have. You know a man is good if you
pretend to be hurt and they become nice. And
wouldn't you know it he was hurt that he hurt
me. 'Look,' he said. 'I am just writing an idea I
have for a book, that's all.' 'Well what's it called.
What's it about.' 'Its called Death and George
Jones. Its a romantic tragedy.' 'The title is a
tragedy,' I said. He smiled. 'Well its something I
have always wanted to try. You know, see if I
could make an audience cry.' 'Tell me about it.'
'Do you really want to know?' I thought for a
few seconds. 'Not really, but its a long trip back.
I hope you aren't pitching me an idea. If that's
what this is about. This won't work no matter
how much I like the idea. Hollywood types get

bored real fast.' He smiled and proceeded to tell
me a wonderful story idea." She turned to me
and questioned, "You must know how it goes.
You surely have read the book." I hadn't so again
I lied. I had the concept down. So if she asked for
my ideas about it, I could fib; yet again.
"Anyway," she started with a proud look, "How
did he begin it. OH! yes. It starts out in a bar. An
older bartender just starts to work there.
Something about saving the life of someone in
the mafia, or something. Anyway he befriends a
young man, who happens to be a drunk. Time
passes and the older bartender starts to befriend
the young man. Who happens to be dying of
cancer. It turns out, his pregnant fiancé must
dump him. Her fathers overriding orders. So he
spends his remaining years in a drunken blur.
Never knowing he even had a child, mind you.
So eventually the young man dies. And of course
through out the story, songs by George Jones are
played. At his funeral, 'He stopped loving her
today,' was played. And she shows up. Surprise.
Surprise. The bar tender is one of his pal-bear-
ers, along with some other drunk regulars. And
as the proceedings go along. there isn't a dry eye
in the funeral home. Except for this bar tender,
who quietly poises a smile. The regulars notice
this. And when they get back to the bar. A toast

to this fine young heartbroken man. They toast and one of the regulars ask. 'Why did you smile?' And his response was. 'I thought of him dancing with his love to 'Tennessee Whiskey.' Of course he told more." She ended the sentence and started coughing severely. I froze. All I could muster was, "are you alright?" Her hand opened a compartment, unseen earlier, and pressed a button. Mrs. Gloria burst in the room and with nurturing hands. Brought her from the fit. She then turned to me, as she guided my Grandmother to her feet, and said. "Sir, we must continue this another time. Tomorrow, if she's feeling better." I stood up finally and watched as she was taken into what must have been her bedroom.

Walking down the series of halls, trying to remember my way out, I heard a voice beckon me. I turned to see Mrs. Gloria. She rushed toward me. My heart sank. I blurted, "should I call an ambulance?" "No. No. That's not why I called to you. Its your Grandmother, she is deathly afraid that you will print that she is in bad health." "Of course I won't." "I know, but she insisted that you be told. The press has scared her." I drooped my head, with a nod of approval and continued my journey. I glanced back to see

Mrs. Gloria rush in the opposite direction. I figured to ease my grandmother's troubled mind.

I tossed and turned in my bed that night. I pondered her condition. 'Should I tell her the truth?' 'Will I finish this book,' the selfish part of me asked. 'Will she die.' I tried to put such nonsense out of my head. Finally sleep came in small doses.

The next day

I went through the same mannerisms as the previous day. Only now I had a face and voice to haunt me. I pictured things she might say. Spasms that may occur. It was even harder. As the water warmed my face in the shower. I couldn't help but to think of Julie. And the time she almost bought the bullet, so to speak. It was a warm spring day. Love was in the air. Squirrels were have sex on the streets, putting on a pornographic show for busy un-attentive students. Julie an I walked hand in hand, down a near by road. No where in particular was our destination. Just free spirited talk. Plans for an uncertain future. Sidewalk steps below our feet. The campus and surrounding surroundings were carefree and crime free. That was a reason father wanted me there. Cars past. A distant police siren in the background, that we took for granite as being a random speeder. The sirens kept blaring and approached. Still our impulsive jabber went forth. When the sirens were just behind and people started to yell and scream, life slowed. Gunshots rang out in random directions. I pulled Julie to the ground. But not before a bullet, that went astray, hit her upper left shoulder. I panicked. I screamed. I was a hysterical husband. One police officer pulled over. I can't remember his words, for the deafness, as he struggled to break our bond. I just saw her laying there trying uselessly to retain the clasp of my hand, as the officer pulled me away and pushed me back. He quickly went down to her as my eyes flooded. I knew love at that moment. I knew of an immense loss impending. I touched my face, caressing it with her blood. Our eyes still locked. After an eternity the ambulance arrived and we scrabbled to the hospital. I knew in the tiny compartment vehicle she was to be alright. Trained men and women made sure of that. Luckily the bullet went clean through. But it was a turning point of our relationship, which for those short moments were to change it forever. I never looked at her the same after that. I think she felt a distantness. I guess life is made up of two people. Those who love and lose and those who die and regret un-loss. We were opposites on that fence. Maybe she thought that I had opened up to much, with my tears. As close as we were that tragic event revealed to much of me. It left her with all the cards. Or possibly it was destiny saying we were meant to be together. And it scared the shit out of me. Oh! And the cops killed the bad guys! The criminal, luckily for them, died a quick death!!

Cold water sprung me out of my flashback trauma and I gasped. After my usual primping and preening I was out the haven toward a second journey into hell. I kept my head down all the way. Trying not to think of anything particular. Just my fast feet. Before I knew it I was rapping the door. Seeing Mrs. Gloria's face. "Your back, well come on in. She's been expecting you." "Is she doing alright?" "Yes she's in fine spirits, how are you? We both kind of wondered if you'd be back." "I am alright I guess," I said during a long yawn. And surprisingly I did feel alright. I guess it was because she was alright and wanted me back.

As I opened the door, I saw her figure as a shadow, gracefully dancing to some old opera tune. Her white gown made her movements all the more classic. When her face noticed mine, I did not see embarrassment or guilt of her primatic shuffle. Just a lost look. But again a soft smile greeted me. And we sat and talked. I took out my micro cassette recorder. And she gently scanned it. "Is this a problem?" "NO dear, I just marvel at technology progress. How everything gets smaller and bigger at the same time." After a long pause her face came back to me, from the fire glow. "So what shall we talk about today? Where did we leave off yesterday? OH! yes. The George Jones and Death. Well I was so entranced by this young man, my senior by a few years. I had to hear more of his thoughts. Good writers are hard to get opened up. The ones I have known are always so quiet or drunk. Or loud and obnoxious. He had a gentile wit and wisdom, that made my heart feel new. So of course we started having dinner. I delayed a film because of him. But the one thing that really sticks out in my mind is the night when destiny took hold. When he laid all the cards in my hand and gave me full rights to a poker face. The night when he confessed the trick that had been pulled on me. It seems my pilot was related to this young Mr. Durham. And was tipped off to the departure. Of course he wasn't a rock climber. And though he did believe in writing at different locations, never on such altitudes. At first I don't think it bothered me, but I pretended it did, for pretending's sake. I acted as if I was mad. Though I didn't yell or rave. He could feel the distantness I was giving off. And he became a desperate man. Contrary to popular belief, woman don't always hate this pathetic form of controlling change. As he was down on his knees, having given up any chance I wouldn't walk out the door. I turned to him and smiled and said, 'aren't I a fabulous Actress?' That night was the most passionate night I had ever known. We made love like strangers on some island longing for someone's touch." I tried to compose my face from the involuntary convulsions that had to come. I so felt like saying, Grandmother! It's me your Grandson, please don't tell me that. I am getting sick. 'Oh, well you know how it goes?'" I snapped back to reality. "What? You weren't paying attention to a thing I said were you?'" Her face showed the expression of wisdom, as mine showed embarrassment of a Journalist not listening. "I can't blame you. I was young once and never cared for talk of the erotic elderly." Her smile and quick wit made a laugh burst from me that just wouldn't stop. And before I knew it we were both laughing uncontrollably.

After catching our breaths' and reflecting with seconds ago nostalgia, she began again. 'Do you want to hear about the video he did for George W. Bush?' I knew the video. In that I had watched it once many years ago. Never had I

heard the story. "Yes. Yes I would." Her gaze
again went to the fire and her neck made a
motion as to swallowing. "This of course was
after we had been a couple for quite sometime.
Those horrific days changed this Country forever. People, in droves, ran to give blood. They
opened their wallets wishing they had more to
give. Bi-Partisan politics was almost a contradic-
tion in terms. There was one Government, no
two sides. We both gave both blood and money.
Then the handsome Mr. Bush came on the T.V.
as he did often and asked for Hollywood's help.
In those weeks after my husband had an idea,
'they would want a few good propaganda's.'
Every time I think of that chose of words he
used, I think of the old man in the goatee, you
know, 'I want you for the U.S. Army.' Anyway, he
got as much footage of President Bush and that
bastard Osama, as he could. And spliced them
together with the soundtrack of 'TOOLS,'
'Sober.' It was all the rage. It showed a man of
morals taking on an enemy in the shadows. The
beginning of the song sounds like something
you'd hear in an Apocalypse Now Helicopter. Do
you know what I mean? Have you seen that
movie. The part I am referring to is when Robert
Duval plays that instrumental music. To scare
the enemy. And of course it was so cool. Oh,

well. If you haven't seen it. I highly recommend
it." I thought about the video and that had never
occurred to me. I must watch it tonight I
thought. But something else I was dying to get
to. Her thoughts about Grandfather's run for
Presidency. "Mrs. Durham can you tell me
about. What most sticks out in your mind about
his run for the highest office?" She smiled. Again
she waited to answer. I guess phrasing correctly
was crucial. "It would have to be when we were
running late for the First Lady debate. I was
nervous, shuffling papers. Trying to think of
attacks my counter-part, Sandra Yelding, might
pull. He was calm and cool though. Maybe that
was why I was nervous. He just knew he was
going to win. He was ahead in the polls. Oozing
with charisma. I was afraid I would make a mistake and ruin it for him. He just sat there in that
Limo as I fussed and stared out the window with
a smile. I remember turning to him and saying
something like, 'what have you got planned. Is
that why your so confident?' My biggest fear was
Sandra would start early. I figured she would say
something like, 'Actresses shouldn't be First
Lady's, they want to hold up peoples valuable
time, by being fashionably late.' And I was right
when we pulled in she was at the podium,
sounding off. Telling the people what was true."

Those last sarcastic words showed a deep resentment she still held. "Then wouldn't you know it. Her husband came up on stage. He wasn't supposed to do that. The crowd cheered. But my husband was confident. He held me back from marching up on stage and ranting. At this point we were in the tech. booth. Now Sandra's husband was not a pure blood citizen of this Country. They enacted a law allowing none born U.S. citizens to run awhile back. The Senate and Congress thought it showed diversity. Which I believe is true. Finally after Mr. Yelding got done trashing my husband. His wife came back and demanded to know were I was. Then it happened, the end of their White House hopes. My husband gave a C.D. to one of the tech. persons and grabbed some of his secret service men. He whispered in my ear, 'let me introduce you.' I gave him a weird little smile. All of the sudden, Mrs. Yelding's micro-phone went blank of words. A big screen behind her started showing an image of him walking toward the stage, with bodyguards in tow, to Bruce Springsteen's 'Born In the U.S.A. The crowd went nuts. The Yelding's faces were red. And I laughed. Boy did I laugh. After minutes and minutes of feet standing applause. My husband echoed these words. 'You ma'am are no Tony

Blair. Lady's and Gentlemen, your next first Lady.' And I made my way down the isle, smiling. The rest, of course is history."

We sat there awhile in silence. My eyes traveled the room and came across the baseball artifact. I turned to her softly. "Tell me about the baseball, on the mantel. If you don't care." She, again, had that far off, unsteady look. She rose rather quick and gracefully. Her hands went to the baseball carefully, as if it could be hot, or dangerous. When the ball was in her palm her eyes squinted and a cracking smile showed mischief. "I keep this ball. Because it always makes me remember of his insane spontaneity. It all started early in his Presidency. He received a call from a prominent Lady New York Senator. It went something like this."

"The phone rang in the freshman President's office. He answered to hear a known voice on the other end, a Mrs. Hillary Clinton. As you know her major hidden agenda was universal health care. Quite the evil scheme, that's sarcasm by the way. Anyway she had read about this old woman, Mrs. Robinson, who was caring for a granddaughter, who's family had died in a car accident. The old woman was still to far away from Medicare and she drew just enough money not to be qualified for Government assistance.

The HMO's President happened to be a big supporter of my husbands' party. Johnny was always a softy. Took pity on every hard case. So he made a phone call to this HMO President, a Mr. Edward Walker, if I recall correctly. Mr. Walker was humble and kind. And offered his support, by saying. His company would make sure this kind old lady got her operation. He even said it would be great publicity. But he stalled. Again Johnny called. And called. It got to the point that this Mr. Walker wouldn't accept my husbands' calls. Now anyone else would just say to hell with you. I'll blast you ever chance I get. And this kind old lady will get her operation, somehow. It wasn't life threatening, but in years it could be. So my husband with his unlimited capabilities, had a wire tap placed all around this Mr. Walker. But no dirt could be dug up. So one day, weeks later my husband set him up. Mr. Walker was in a board meeting. And my husband called. Though Mr. Walker wasn't to be disturbed, his secretary had enough common sense to know when the President of the United States calls, you answer. As my husband waited listening on the phone with one ear, on the other the wiretap picked up. 'I don't care who it is, I said no calls.' The secretary left to, I assume, to lie to my husband but the phone was dead.

Johnny was more intent now on the wiretap.
'Some damn old lady, who's going to die soon,
wants an expensive operation. The young lad
should know you can't win them all,' Mr. Walker
said as his boardroom applauded his bravery in
the face of anti-capitalistic patriotism. I don't
know how it happened. I wasn't there. Like allot
I have told you, its all second hand. Granted second hand from the horses mouth. When he told
me, before the news blasted it. We were laying in
bed. I was turned to him. Like an interested
child, as he studied some papers. Looking ever
so wise. He said, 'I picked up a bat I had from the
closet and told the secret service I had an errand
to run. We hopped on Air Force One and sooner
than you could imagine we were pulling up in
front of the Insurance company's sky scrapper.
For some reason their meetings must last a long
time. I guess you have to figure there are many
needy people out there that must be ailing, but
it's so costly. A few more dollars are worth more
than several meaningless lives. Before I knew it I
was busting in the office. Staring intently on Mr.
Walker. I demanded everyone leave, naive Mr.
Walker thought this included him as well. I told
him to set down and for his sake, shut up. He
looked at me pleadingly, saying he was so busy.
Really, I said. Busy saving lives, young lad. His

face dropped. Now keep in mind I had a bat. And as I hit him over and over, I screamed, YOU CAN"T AFFORD A DOCTOR!!!!!!! Sticks and stones may break their bones if their words hurt me.'

I lay there mesmerized. Needless to say Mrs. Robinson got her operation. She was invited to the White House and presented Johnny with this autographed baseball of Joe DiMaggio. Of course the press had a field day with that." "With what," I questioned. "The Simon and Garfunkel song."

I vaguely remembered the verses. And it was- n't until later I saw the true irony my Grandfather lived. An ironic life twice lived.

"O.K. I have to know. About Palestine and how the Middle East conflict worked out." She made her way back to her seat a bit slower, after carefully returning the baseball to its position. 'Those times were difficult. The whole world was on the brink of another World War. People showed the same patriotism as they showed in the first few days of the Enduring Freedom Conflict. Instead of pushing and shoving to get gas. They were fighting and in some cases killing to get food. Martial law was imposed, but every- one. It was almost like they reveled in the panic. The thrill. Some prayed to Jesus. Others got away with viciousness so horrible I dare not return to it. And my husband, my lucky, brave, dumb-ass husband. He retired. Handed over the reigns of power to the Vice-President. His final order was to find the nearest white hot air balloon.' "Why that. I mean why a hot air balloon? I mean I understand now. But did he give you any clue?" "No I don't even think he did until his mind sprung it on him. He just kissed me good-bye. Never told me where he was going. He just made sure his family was in a safe place. For some reason none of the Secret Service knew how to fly a hot air balloon. So the owner had to fly it. The owner, by the way, was Tommy Chong. It was loaded on Air Force One and flew as close to the waiting battlefield as it could possibly get. On board the plane, a massive sound system was installed. So it could blast out music or a speech. At the time I doubt if He knew what was about to occur.'"

She stopped talking long enough to bring a drink of some soft drink to her lips, which rested on her opposite side, out of my site. She let it go down slowly. She finished it abruptly and started to cough. As I arose to give aide she stopped and motioned me back to my seat. I obliged her order. She sat there looking and listening to the crackling of the fire. When another fit of coughing hit. Again her hand went to some dark void and pulled what could have only been some hand held panic button. And with each cough she ferociously pounded it. I went to her just as Mrs. Gloria came to her aide. "Help me help her into bed." I quickly went around the opposite side of her and lifted half of her frail body. We carried her into a bedroom and laid her down. The whole time I felt her eyes on me. Judging whether I was judging her. "We'll have to finish up tomorrow," she whispered loudly. My eyes left her in shame, and they caught Grandfather in different shapes and sizes all about from floor to ceiling. In no order young here a little older there. A false God shrine of memorabilia.

I found myself in bed, thinking about the day's events, as I tried not to. I needed a break. But I pushed myself to listen to the tape of what transpired. The hard things are easier to remember, that's all I thought of as I heard her words repeated from the micro-cassette recorder; but in the back of my mind it was that retched hacking of her withered lungs.

Like usual though, as of late, if I wasn't thinking about one woman; it was another. Julie lay in the hospital, in a colorless room on a lifeless bed. I peered through her window and watched her laugh with her parents. She occasionally turned to meet my gaze only to find it turn quickly. A bullet had torn us apart and she was still alive. As much as I didn't want to lose her I knew I had. I screwed it up. She wasn't asking for tears or gushing love spewed out. She just wanted a man that would hold her hand. Make her laugh. And I knew this the whole time. We stayed together until some few previous nights ago. We never spoke of the bullet. She saw something inside of me that she thought she could bring about into the light. But I was too much of a macho man. I couldn't show her the love I had for her. I couldn't tell her that something inside of me yearned for her so strongly that I couldn't come close to describing. I couldn't show her in actions that I wanted to become deaf in an eternity kiss. I couldn't do a damn thing but nothing. And in my heart, over time, I knew I couldn't expect her to except that. She deserved the world. And I deserved the regret of always wishing that I could have said something, while her body ached, like, "Will you marry me?"

I woke the next day feeling forlorn but with purpose. The evening was approaching and I could see Grandmother didn't have much longer. I could see it in her eyes and in her actions from the previous day and this day didn't change her dreary outlook. I found myself again setting in the same chair waiting for her words, armed with my micro-cassette recorder, staring at her pale green gown. "Now where were we," she questioned the ceiling. "Oh yes. The hot air balloon. I really can't do anything but speculate any further what went through his mind as he went through the motions. It was just simple. Palestinians and Jews were lined up, kind of like in our Civil War. I guess about twenty feet apart, not close enough to spit on each other. Yelling and cursing each other, though. It must have been an act of GOD, or maybe they were really more scared than they made out to be. But they waited. Maybe they were waiting for a miracle. And boy did it come. From the clouds came this hot air balloon. Blasting what non English speaking people would call opera. What others would call a song from the movie 'O Brother, Where Art Thou?' called "Down To The River To Pray." He spoke elegantly Saying things like, 'What right do you have to instill hate into your children? Do you want them to die? Does OUR GOD want hatred? Where does it preach that? We have had tough lives, everyone. One thing that's wrong is the television exposure. Lets stop this nonsense. Or do it. Just kill each other. But start

with the children first. Line them up and shoot
them in the heads. Then on the count of three.
Blast each other away. Then right before GOD
sends you all to hell, you can demand of god.
'Who's right?'" And with those chose words,
peace finally followed. That and a promise of my
husband to set up a company that would
employ all jobless Palestinians. My son now
takes care of that." "So you have no idea if all
those movies and such about what went
through his mind while on that hot air balloon
were right?" "Goodness no. He never spoke of it.
Tommy Chong never spoke of it either. But they
remained friends. He was a Pal Bearer when he
died. Maybe it was to spiritual to share with the
world. Who knows?"

I was satisfied and wondered if I should push
it by asking about the potheads Bob an Arnold.
I bit my tongue and took the chance. I know
people in politics don't usually like to discuss
marijuana, but I have to ask," and I pointed to
them. She smiled as she shook her head. "GOD,
those two idiots. Why them? Anyone but
them." "Come on tell me." "All this talk is bring-
ing back memories of dread. Over and over."
"Your not getting out of it that easy," I rebuked.
She sighed and gave a waning smile. It was just
months before that fateful bullet took him. The

Vice-President decided to let Johnny run again. That's what the World wanted. The Vice-President of course stayed on as the second in command for four more years. Anyway he was giving a speech.......I forgot where he was giving that speech. I remember it was some University. And Bob an Arnold, both students, helped to erect the stage. The Secret Service kept a watchful eye on them. Obviously two stoners. There was a man there." Her face took on a post traumatic look. "Some type of waiter or something. No one knows how he managed to get the gun in. But all of the sudden he was running. Running toward the stage as my husband was giving a speech. My husband didn't even know a man was running from behind the curtain toward him. The Secret Service agent closest to Johnny slipped. But there was Bob. In his cat swiftness. It was incredible the speed, Bob exerted. He jumped between Johnny and the gun. The gun fired but no one was hurt of course. Arnold was a few steps behind and picked up the pistol and fired it into the guys legs, saying matter-of-factly, 'you shouldn't have done that, bad, bad, bad assassin.' The Secret Service took the gun from Arnold. My husband was whisked back to the safe house, where I was in tears. We hugged and he asked for the two young gentlemen, who were apparently brought in a car there as well. They were brought in. My husband was a little taken aback. This was the first he had seen who had done the heroic act. They had long hair. Arnold I think had a t-shirt that said 'Johnny smoked pot, he's our hero.' He stood looking at them with his arm around me, with a 'what the hell is this' look on his face. I looked at them as sons, through my tears. Then they talked. It was very short, something like. 'Hey man, want to get drunk?' Johnny just shook his head. Said thank you and they were gone. But not without a reward. The press ate them up." We sat there awhile. Not saying anything. And then I asked. "Do you want to talk about his assassination?" She took a deep breath. I waited for her response for quite some time then finally I said, "it really doesn't matter." I got about half way up from my seat when she began. "I had reservations about him going out that day. Riding along in a convertible down a main street strip. It was too similar to J.F.K., he told me that. He said that was why I was so nervous. But the hypocrite in him wouldn't let me ride along. Sometimes I wish I did. I could have been there for him, or maybe I could have died as well. I might has well have died that day too. I just haven't been the same since. Some have dared to ask if I regret this isolation, would this be want he would want of my life? Before he left we had a fight. A meaningless fight. I wanted a broach I had seen. He refused. I was so mad.......... We would always kiss before he did something so simple but so dangerous as going out in public. But I didn't kiss him. No matter how much I worried about him. I wouldn't let go of that selfishness. I remember watching him. The car slowly driving along..........then." Her eyes squeezed shut and she jumped a little. "BANG! BANG! I saw him lifeless. I saw myself without him. They say that a person sees their life flash before their eyes when they die. I saw my life do that. I saw him on that mountain, smiling. With Vince Gill singing, "On The Mountain." I saw us dancing at the Inaugural with my red dress on to that Chris DeBurg song. I thought about the fight we had over some meaningless broach, which I later found he had gotten me anyway. There were many songs done, little videos composed to celebrate his life. Elton John sang his third and final installment of "Candle in the Wind." "Only Time." "I hope you had the time of your life." "Goodbye to Romance." "My Heart will go on." The Elton John song I will remember the most. Our Grandson had just been hatched, not to long before all that. It was here." She pointed to the wall. "Outside in that direction, where the memorial stands. Elton sang it. Fireworks lit up the sky. My Grandson said his first words that day. I remember smiling, the first time I had smiled in such a long while. I saw a little bit of Johnny in him. He pointed with his little fingers to the statue, looked at me and said 'Pap-paw'."

I put my head down to cover the tears. That, something, deep in me wanted her to talk more of me. Say something like, 'when I see this Grandson again I will hug him and forgive him of his sin in not seeing me after all this time.' But none of that came. I cleared my throat. My few days with Grandmother were over. Would I reveal my true identity, I hadn't a clue. Deep down I knew I would, I had to......someday. "I guess that's enough. I'll come by tomorrow, if you don't care and get a few last words." "What more do you need?" My back was to her now and the well of emotion ran to strong for me to talk much more. "I don't know off hand, I am sure there will be something." My last lie to her. I couldn't wait to get out of that room, like I couldn't bear going into Julie's hospital room. "There's just one final thing," she said. "What's that?" "I forgive you Grandson." The waterworks fell. "I am sorry Grandma. I am so sorry" I turned and ran to her seat, fell on my knees and cried on her lap, begging her forgiveness. She stroked my hair. All I could think about was how I had missed so much. And how I thanked GOD for letting me hear her say those words. The tears were such a load off. "I have something else to tell you," she said in between my tears. Her smile was warm and passionate. "I am a good actress, aren't I reporter?" I was dumbfounded. My face was a mass of confusion. "What?" "I'm not dying. I just told them to say that because it was the only way to get you to visit." My mouth dropped open and my body was pushed back from her knee. She jumped up with the spirit of a teenager. "Now come on lets get out of these rooms." "Are you saying you do leave the house?" "Sometimes, I am not a hermit. Give me some credit."

We had dinner that evening and laughed and didn't say one word about Grandfather. We made up for lost time. And though it was great talking to her. There was this other woman I couldn't get off my mind that I had wronged.

I stared out the window of my bedroom. In my line of sight was the statue of Grandfather, many of you have seen. Whether in a book or in real life. 'What would you say Grandfather?' I said aloud. Give me some lovely love wisdom so new it must be centuries old, I thought. Was it to late? Julie. Julie. If we had went our entire twelve years of school together I would have known you were the one in second grade. I would write you a love letter now even if I knew you would throw it into a fire. What do I say to someone whom I ache for? How do I make up for being a complete asssssssssssss? How do I run into that hospital and leave your face wet with kisses? How do I look you in the eyes and say 'I am sorry?' Then it hit me. I knew exactly what to do. And like when we were new at love, it was the 'just right thing' to say.

Grandmother's lie

The next morning father woke me and told me the bad news. She had died the previous night, outside in the moonlight. Underneath Grandfather's statue. Beside her was a stereo that had Ozzie's, 'Goodbye to Romance,' on repeat. Grandmother had died the night we became family once more. I didn't mourn when the coroner came. I didn't mourn when I saw the black bag that carried her body. I smiled. Sure I regretted not making her acquaintance sooner. But I pictured her, in a red gown, with a man I now admire even more greatly; dancing to some old George Jones' song. I called Julie and left her a message on the answering machine. It went something like, 'I have something you must read before it's published.'

And to you, the reader. The moral of THIS story is. So what if this book is not perfectly punctuated or if it didn't go the way you'd hoped, or if it's to short. I am new at this remember? It's my story. Love it or hate it, there're just words. Words below a micro-cassette recorder lying on a star spangled flag.

ON LATER EXAMINATION

◆

My father, mother an I, days after her funeral, went through the tedious task of excavating grandmother's things. To my surprise and to you, the readers; what luck. I stumbled across his journal. It's not long. Probably about as long as the preceding story. I guess its short because he never really had the time to do any writing. About his personal self. Outside of his fictional works. Which I dare say express his life, put in different format and left as mystery to understand. But its his first hand account of perspective, thought to be long evaporated in the many sun shiny days that have past after his death. A sun that best expresses time, that has gloomed so many. But yet has inspired to this day. I left it unedited, like my story. You will find no revelations. No predictions of death. No ancient knowledge that will unlock mystery's. Just the story of a boy who quested to become a man. So without any further ado.

I decided to start this journal out of shear boredom. This handwritten account of my life so far is meant for many reasons. Illegitimate children being one reason. I will probably get into other reasons later, when you discover the depths of arrogance that lie in me. The boredom comes from the electricity being out and being a child brought up by the GOD television. A night under the glow of the moon shall be something new, for as Brandon Lee said, "You never know how many times in your life you may see it. Maybe twelve times at most, but its limitless." I am paraphrasing but its true, and those words still give me goose bumps. So I will write until I decide to finish. One long run -on sentence is probably what will emerge.

I was born in the month of Julius. On that day the Doctor had me sent to the big city hospital because of a bump on my head. I was told at five months I was the star attraction in a church play. With no words I peacefully laid in a manger. My preteen years far behind. I can barely recall happiness. I stayed with a baby-sitter, before catching the bus to school, and who's oldest Granddaughter daughter hurt me. Not physically of course. But mentally. Always showing her spiteful looks. Saying hate filled things.

The only instance I can recall was one morning waiting for the bus. And hearing her rant and rave. Her words still hurt to this day. She said something along the lines of, 'your parents are so old. Your lucky your not a retard.' Their hatred grew for me. The only times I enjoyed going to the house was before Christmas break. When I gave them presents. At the age of twelve I finally got to leave the house. And have only spoken to them a few times since. Of course at that time I was starting Junior high. Which wasn't much better. The teachers at that school were mean. And as at the baby-sitter's, they were only nice come breaks. I guess they were mean because they hated getting up early. That first year, seventh grade, I became a hypochondriac. Everyone seemed to like me but I was lonely. In those years, I remember for my birthday my brother-in-law called and invited me to a base-ball card show in a surrounding town. On the phone I heard him ask my sister if she wanted to come. She said, 'not if he's going.' I heard his stammering. I knew he knew I heard the comment. And I hung up. Now my sister rode to work with my parents and they of course dropped me off at the evil baby-sitter's. I was always a guy that would hold things in. Except for this day. When I saw her get in. I did my best to totally ignore her. When she brushed against me I pulled away, like she was a disease. As I got out of the tiny Chevy hatchback I again did something to provoke. She asked what the hell my problem was and at that moment I changed. Massively but not too much to look back now, in that that innocent me, I no longer recollect. I screamed at her. I ranted. I could feel my face change with the hate I spewed forth. In those few minutes I replayed for her everything she had ever done that hurt me, up until that birthday insult. I think I remember tears in her eyes. As she just sat there and took it. My parents didn't say a word. From that day forth. I recall a calmer sister. At least around me. I also don't remember her riding in with my parents to work anymore. I bare no ill will toward my sister, she has tried hard to be a sister to me. But I am an only child. That's how I have always felt.

Eighth grade wasn't much better teacher wise. They were still mean. But I was damned if I was going to continue not seeing friends at the cost of some assholes who hated their life and lived by the code of school; no talking, social isolation. But one instance I do remember. The week of Halloween we had dress up days. On one particular day, sixties day. When everyone dressed like they were hippies. I dressed like I

was in my sixties. Cane an all. Final class was
Science. This teacher, I think hated me the
most; out of all the teachers I had had. Anyway.
I had stupidly let a friend who was prone to getting in trouble see my cane. She came in an
announced that it was her cane now. My father's
belt expressed his disapproval. Years later on the
phone with an old friend, Perry, who was a
grade under me. He revealed that another evil
teacher said something bad to him. He had finished his assignment and asked to look at his
friend's sunglasses. His immature mind made
the comment to loud that they were cool. The
teacher promptly said, 'I pity the woman who
marries you.' I couldn't believe she had said
that. But then again I could. He also told me
about some poor child in his class who had to
leave school one day because of a severe
headache. The evil Science teacher made the a
smart-ass comment that went something like,
'he does have something wrong with his head.'
The next day, come to find out, he was in a
coma. And Perry said as far as he knew he still
was. So that day she said something like, 'I want
to apologize to you all. It just goes to show. You
have to watch the things you say.' Now keep in
mind that this was ten years later that this conversation took place between me and Perry. By

then I had already finished my first book. And knew I had an amazing gift for the written word. But I couldn't let things go. Still I have that problem to this day. I wanted vengeance. For me, Perry and that poor coma kid. Now keep in mind. This was during the time of the idiots of Columbine and other school shootings. And I wanted to send a none violent message to my attacker. So I did something worse than a bullet could ever do. I wrote a letter. I demanded my cane back. I was so eloquent and spiteful by the time I was done I was breathing hard. I even threw the old line teachers use on bullies that went something like this. "There's an old teachers saying. Don't pick on him or her they could be your boss one day. Its a pity you hypocrites can't practice what you preach." Under where I signed my name. I typed The Count Of Monte Cristo. Did I get a response to that letter? Of course. It just was and wasn't what I had expected. The Principal wrote me back a very crafty letter. And you know what. I don't think about those evil people anymore. And there has since been no school shootings. I do worry about myself sometime. That letter so unburdened me. I gave that hate back to its rightful place. But I know she will never forget it. Of course maybe she isn't as mean as she once was. Maybe the school is a more kinder place. Maybe children can learn without fear. A fear thrust upon me.

High-school was a breath of fresh air. I lost weight by playing basketball all summer. From morning to night. I rarely ate. I just shot for hours upon hours by myself. And as the day before my first day came. I cut my hair. Bought more normal clothes and determined myself to conform my appearance and left my mind wonder as it always has. That first day was scary. Hearing horrible stories of how the lowly ninth grader was destined to be beaten to a pulp. Or worse yet humiliated in front of beautiful girls. But none of that came. And as the day ended I found my ass being pinched by the hottest senior in school. That tall blonde vixen with bright blue eyes made coming to school and getting my education worthwhile again.

I quickly befriended the senior class with my deranged vocal sense of humor. And a daring that left teachers who should have punished me, jaw dropped and head shaking. Those were truly the best times in my life. Everyone liked me. I was one, if not the, most popular kid in my class. I was readily invited to parties and found the taboo of drug taking to be ridiculous. Though I will talk more of that later. That inaugural year I also found a girl I'll call M. M was stunning. The most popular girl in class. Blonde hair blue eyes. Fantastic figure. We flirted allot. And when Valentine's Day came, I found myself doting her with the most expensive. I spent about fifty dollars alone on the candy. But in all that time I never asked her out. Looking back now I guess. I wanted her, but not enough to be looked upon as a couple. I was nowhere ready for a high-school hand holding marriage. We finally became just friends I guess when I was walking down the hall one day and felt a hand gently grab mine. I quickly pulled away for, I guess, fear of some homosexual thingy. We looked at each other in horror. She said something like, 'I just wanted to hold your hand.' I told her my hand hurt. She just looked down sad eyed. I couldn't just tell her the truth. I couldn't say. "My palms are sweaty. And I care to much about you to have you think I am anything but perfect." No I couldn't say that. OH! well. I am comforted in the fact that she married, after high-school, a super nice guy. I am happy that she found happiness with someone who will love her and never hurt her. What else could a man who loves someone want more than the obvious?

My sophomore year I remember little about. But my Junior year brought Scott. Now this guy was something else. He was a real DOG, and I say that with profound respect. This guy loved women. I think he loved collecting them more than loved them, however. And he was ripped. For a high-school student he was in great shape. He introduced me to some older friends. Which now I think of as my original bad influences. I mean I was a Junior hanging with guys twenty-four or so. And they readily took me as a protégé. But I may talk about them more later. One moment sticks out in my mind most about Scott. At one time he was dating this girl from a surrounding county. She was a bit younger than us and wild. I mean really wild. I'll call her E. One night Scott came and picked me up and said me, him, E an another of our friends were going to camp out. I had nothing better to do, so I willingly succumbed to his demand. When we arrived E was well on her way to being completely hammered. Our friend wanted to leave and I was asked to baby-sit. Immediately her advances started. But I was an original I said no. She even had the gall to jump on me in the tent in front of Scott. Why did she do this you ask? Was it because of my stunning looks? Yes! But more so because I let them have sex in my bed, while I laid next to them. Urging them to control their moans, for my parents where in the bedroom next door. When they finished she turned on her side and spooned up to me. How should I explain what happened next? I guess the best way to put it is. While E and Scott talked. E's moon successfully rose my rocket. After they broke up. She came by my house one day with a few other guys. They invited me to a party. I went and was told she wanted me bad. My chances were ruined when E asked me to rub her feet and I couldn't because they stunk. Last I knew E was pregnant. Now in fifth period Scott and I sat near each other. And he always pestered me about one girl I became friends with in the ninth grade, who I will call T. She had moved from the city school and started talking to me. I guess because the class we were in we knew absolutely no-one. I guess I should have mentioned her sooner, but OH! well. We started talking one day. I was pretty mute. I just let her talk. I wonder to this day why I wasn't more vocal with her. She was stunning. Another of my Blonde hair blue eyed beauties. Incredibly petite. Not an ounce of fat anywhere. Anyway the day I started paying attention to her was when she told about her and another beauty I went to school with, I'll call her Q. She said when they were over at either of their respected houses. They would, take compromising pictures of each other. Of course for a boy of my limited age and over active imagination. This was enough to start a friendship that to this day I miss not getting more of. She was kind enough to give me a picture of Q. She wouldn't however give me a picture of her. The picture was dark, but Q was naked, holding her breasts in a provocative way. She got mad when I asked if there was any below the waist shots. Which I found quite comical and so womanly. Tease a little and then claim sexual harassment. I mean isn't that reverse sexual harassment? Putting the image in my head and then, you know. How did I get here? Oh! Scott pestering me. Well as I said I sat with Scott and friends on one side of the room. She sat on the other. One day in question coming back from lunch. Which I now remember was close to the end of the year. She started grabbing my ass as we walked down the hall, coming back from lunch. It was just me, Scott, and her. Anyway in the class T propositioned me. She said tomorrow her teacher for some class was taking them to the beach and she would be wearing her bathing suit. She said if I showed her my naked chest today she would show me her bikini top tomorrow. I stood there for a moment, thinking about it. When Scott brought me back to my senses by saying something like, 'what are you waiting for?' So I did. The next day rolls around as did fifth period. On the way back from lunch I was alone. I didn't expect her to show me anything. And when I saw her with Q smile at the doorway and signal me with her index finger. I leapt from my seat to give chase. They took me in an empty room. And she bared her sternum. I was in shock. She was so thin. I had no idea she had anything much to look at. Man was I surprised. I think I commented on that thought. She moved back to her old school after that year. She was probably the first I ever thought of in that way as a friend. It's hard to be in love with someone and only later grasp that paradox. Oh! well.

With senior year of high-school came relief of twelve years of education but also a sadness that so many faces would only be a memory thought of over drunken nostalgia of what I didn't do. That first day of school when I got my schedule I noticed a major mistake. It had me down for only three classes instead of the usual six. I assumed correctly that someone somewhere in the administration thought I was co-oping. And since it was there mistake I could easily let them live with it, as I would have no problem. My first class was Political Science. The teacher had a reputation for being mean. But I found him to be a very good teacher. I remember one Sunday. Some of my friends and I were parked at a popular drug refuge on the side of an old road. Little did I know this teacher of Political Science lived down that road. And as luck would have it, when the joint touched my lips he passed by and saw. He turned back around and shook his head in disgust. Suffice to say, we left quickly. The next few days in school were awkward. But he never said anything. Finally one day came along and he had the class all laughing and discussing something I dare say I wasn't aware of then. When he looks at me and says something to the effect of, 'I've passed stuff around before.' I smiled and my fading paranoia vanished. Second period was English. The only thing I remember about that class was coming in on one of the first days wired from my first experience with cocaine and two strippers. I promise I will get more into that later.

As for third period. That was the class I was to co-op out of. I don't recall the class title but it had to do with business. And we opened a popular brand named grocery store inside. For the students of course. I was head of security. The teacher of the class was a wonderful woman, who was more like a favorite aunt than one who instructs. And there was also H and S. They were some more of my blued eyed phillies. I remember taking S one time to the main grocery store to get more supplies. She rode on the cart as I pushed from behind. That was one of those memorial erotic moments. But of course I said nothing to her either.

As for H. She was special. Now I will be the first to say. I AM A WALKING CONTRADIC-TION! I am shy around women, but can be very out spoken. And H evolved me into that. Or maybe it was just because she was so easy to be with. But as I was saying, I could sexually harass her freely. She enjoyed it. It was fun. And she would do the same to me. Small teases. On a fieldtrip one day the class had its picture taken and because of the limited space we all had to back up as far as we could. Of course H was in front of me. You get what I am saying. I wish that picture could have lasted a thousand years.

As for co-oping without a job. I was eventu-ally figured out and made to tend to the grocery store. Which I didn't mind. It gave me time to reflect and kept me away from drugs which had started to become an everyday thing at this point. Actually it was just one drug; Marijuana.

Now on the third Wednesday of every month we would gather in our homeroom class and wait to be called to our respected clubs. I was in the Business club with my third period teacher. And while I waited. There was D. And like me she had brown hair and brown eyes. Stunningly beautiful. She had a smile that could warm you as a mother would stroke a frightened child's hair. But she also had a temper that required little to set off. And more than once I was the victim of punches. Although I didn't do anything, most times. Seriously, I would just walk in and she would be mad and take it out on me. I always figured it was her way of exercising sexual tension and frustration. And you know what? I think I was right! I had her pegged for marriage in kindergarten. Or there about. Whenever we gazed at each other there was something there, though we didn't look into each other's eyes for long periods.

Then one day on a field trip, an underclassman who was in my third period class came up to me and gave me a revelation that caused my heart to patter and ego to soar. He related the news that as I was walking by her and he. D had pulled him close and whispered that I had a nice ass. Which was true. From that day forward it was tight pants ,and GQ poises; when she was around. I vividly recall one Wednesday setting across from her. The chairs were aligned in a U. I sat on one side and she on the other. Anyway. I happened to be wearing shorter than normal shorts that particular day. When I realized I hadn't looked at her in some time I looked up to see her staring at me. Though not at my eyes. I thought for a second she must be staring at the ground below my feet. So I decided to test this likely theory. I crossed my legs. She looked up at me immediately. Her expression showed a deer CAUGHT in the headlights of an on coming big-rig. And you know what I did? Not a damn thing. I would see her out cruising with her friends on the strip and I could see in her eyes she wanted me to say something but I never did. I would just mirror her look.

Some years later. I had to go to court to pay fines. As it turned out she worked near the Courthouse. I paused and realizing I had money left. I decided to venture past her window of employment and into the pawnshop across the street. I came out with a video but more so, the idea that if she saw me she would give chase. Not to far past her window I heard steps behind me. I didn't know what to say. I turned around to see if it was truly her and it was. But just as quickly I returned my eyes forward. When I looked back again she was gone. She's married now.

The Stripper J. Where do I begin. I guess obviously the beginning. An old friend named Tony called me one day, I think it was my first week of my Senior year of high-school. He had mentioned her prior. On a job interview for a Discount Mart. He saw her. He said she was so unbelievably gorgeous that he fell over a chair watching her instead of where he was going. Anyway. He awakens me from a slumber and asks if I want to accompany him, her and another stripper friend to an "Exotic club" that night. We were both only seventeen. And I had school the following day. Which I figured I would miss if I went. But with little argument I decided it would be unwise not to embark on this adventure of dream like fantasy. Within the hour he arrived at my house and into the back I sat next to the other stripper whom I'll call C. For all of his tall tales Tony was understated at her beauty. Her dark skin, large breast, petite figure, and gleaming blue eyes made me more than quiet. It down right frightened me. And C was so my type. Willing to be spontaneous on a moments notice. She was wild and athletic. She sort of reminded of Lori Petty. Anyway, so we

arrive and watched them dance. Among several
others. When we left at about three in the morning we drove to a house and sat passive as they
downed narcotics. By eight in the morning I was
pissed. I had already missed my first day of
school. I knew my parents would be pissed. And
I sulked at Tony. Who I shouldn't have, I understood then; also. But he did tell me we would be
back in time for my classes. After time J came
out and so did C. C managed to get me out of
my rut by licking my ear and saying we would
get a hotel room and everything would be fine.
Of course we didn't and by ten we were back
home and off to school I went. Wired from the
coke laced joint they told me was harmless. After
my long three periods of class I would go over
there. And sometimes I took a former friend of
mine, whom I'll call S. S is a story unto itself and
will get more into him later. But for now I'll tell
you a little about the night we were over there
together. S and I that is. As we walked through
the door. I was greeted by another stripper,
whom I'll call R. She was tall, blonde, and had
demon tattoos on her buttocks. She pulled me
to the couch and gave me my first lap-dance. As
I sat there enjoying it and watching all the eyes
watch us, she asked, 'do my tit's look funny?' I
said no. Then she said, 'D says my tits look like

German Shepard's.' D by the way was J's younger brother who had moved in. So S an I eventually left. Days later I found I couldn't go back over to the apartment of sin. J's abusive boyfriend had found her and was a very jealous person. He also had won, two years straight, a tough man contest. So they eventually headed back to the big city.

I would sometimes make journeys to see them. One occasion Tony an I went and managed to go out on dates with J and her sister. Her sister whom I'll call A was also a stripper and since Tony was so hung up on J, the lovely and vivacious A was mine. I don't remember how the night turned out though. The only time other than that that I remember being with them. Just me J and A was the first night I ever got anything off smoking crack. They had managed to score some and asked if I would drive them around. They gave me a hit as I was driving down the interstate. And I'll tell you for those few minutes of paranoid bliss, I could see how someone could become addicted to it off the first hit. The rush was powerful. It was like inhaling gas and nitrous-oxide at the same time. For all my coming addictions I am so glad I never got involved with that shit.

On one of the last nights A an I went out and she hurt me. By borrowing an expensive necklace and going off with another guy. I left the big city in a huff. Only to return hours later and retrieve my heirloom. When I was near my home. My mind said to me, 'you need advice.' And literally within seconds my angel appeared. Disguised as a homeless man named Jonathan he gave me wisdom that only your perfect stranger can reveal. On that ride I realized I was in love with J. And I told him about it. For his unknowing help I treated the man who had no more than two dollars in his pocket and hundreds of miles to hitchhike, a meal. As I dropped him at a gas station that lead the route he needed to travel I gave him a piece of advice, 'just remember Jonathan. Remember the Golden Rule.' He winked at me as he took a big bite off his cheeseburger. And I rode off into the sunset. Thinking naively that I was his angel. Only years later did I come to understand he was mine.

With new found energy and purpose I decided to talk to J. Just me and her. We had never been alone more than minutes. But that was about to change. I pursued her. She would flank me with such questions as, 'if your not happy at home why don't you move in with me?'

Or, 'if I asked you to have sex with me would you?' These questions, though asked by the opposite sex, meaning they had probably different meaning than my heart could envision; only fueled my fire of wanting her. Finally the day came. I would finally tell her how I felt. I had never told a woman what I was about to tell this perfect for me person. Late that night, before going home, I told her I had feelings. I even used the phrase everyone has heard, "you complete me." She said she would have to think about it. She said she would call tomorrow. Of course she never did. Two days later as I was pacing around the house I caught my first glimpse of a new Tom Cruise movie. Guess which one!

Years past and I had started my first year of college. And that something inside me would not let the memory of her subside. So with little encouragement from a new friend we ventured to a strip bar in the big city. Now keep in mind all big cities have many strip bars. And as we were having fun at this particular one. I decided once and for all to let the memory of her remain that way. As the hours of morning approached me and my friend, ever the more intoxicated, decided soon we would make our way back home. I wanted one last lap dance from a familiar blue eyed blonde hair. We talked and as the new song started and she mounted me. My heart sank. It was that popular Bruce Springsteen song from, again, guess what movie.

So I made a call and sure enough her and her sister were working, at this particular establishment that they frequented. My friend and I went. I walked in. And A immediately came to me. She guided me to J. And I was surprised and happy that she had gained weight. For that must indicate that crack no longer ruled her every waking moment. We talked and decided to meet the following week.

When I arrived in the big city the following week I stopped at a pay phone and dialed the number. When the bartender handed her the phone it felt like old times. She said, 'call back in an hour.' And promptly got off the phone. I wasn't surprised. I was just indifferent. I no longer loved her. And it had nothing to do with her weight gain. I just realized I had wasted my life pursuing something that I always knew was unattainable bliss. I didn't blame her. She was older than me. She had four children. Women need stability and I was some love struck boy.

So I went to a strip bar near the one she was working at. An hour came and past. Two hours turned to three. I sulked in a corner away from view. Just wanting to contemplate. As the early

morning came I had decided once and for all to
seek the closure I always wanted and was always
denied. I called and when J got on the phone she
sounded ecstatic to hear my voice. I assumed she
figured I would call at one hour to the second.
Instead I left her waiting, finally. I drove to her
club and informed the doorman to tell J and her
sister A, I had arrived. About fifteen minutes or
so later they come out. With some stranger, fellow about my age, in tow. A asked if I could give
him a ride home. After some pestering on their
part I conceded. We went to some house and A
took this fellow to the back room and well, had
sex. At one point she came and got J who went
back there as well. It was at that moment I knew
I could never love someone like this. Finally we
made our exits and I took J to her house. We had
gotten into a fight on the way over. I forget what
about. But she gave me what I wanted to hear.
She said, 'do you know why we could never be a
couple? Because you scare.' And on cue I said,
'well I guess I am just the Anti-Christ.' I always
did have a flare for the dramatic. That was the
last I heard of J. I took the fellow home. And
came to the realization that this fellow, if we had
lived close, would have been my friend. Maybe
my best-friend. I came home and vowed to end
my quest for women. How did I do that you ask.

I became an alcoholic. Which upon inspection now, worked, but should have failed miserably. Meaning that, drunks are best categorized as drinking because they lost the woman they loved. Or their dog was shot. It isn't used for the major purpose of alleviating heartache.

I guess you say, 'so what; love hurts. You were a fool to get involved with a stripper. You were young, naive. Loves out there. You just have to find it.' I heard and knew there was more fish in the sea. But the problem with love is, it blinds you. It makes you do crazy, psychotic things. Things that make you look pathetic. That in turn makes you want to crawl into a hole never to be seen again. Because the bad always shines brighter in people's eyes than the good you have done. I screwed up. I went after the wrong one that I fell for. And maybe even worse than that. I only tried one of the many that I could have been with. But what can you do. Wish hopelessly that you could go back in time and change it? Well yes. But she's out there. I understand that now. And with maturity I know I won't become that blathering fool again. I'll be cautious. I'll control my primal needs. I'll find happiness.

Drugs, where do I begin. My first time with alcohol, which happened to be my freshman year of high-school, was to say the least; unhappy. I hated the taste. But I relented to peer pressure.

The first time I did marijuana I got absolutely nothing. Maybe I wasn't inhaling, who knows. I don't recall when I started enjoying pot. But I did. By Senior year, I was smoking at least a joint a day. Sometimes before school. Which now makes even less sense than it should have then because I was just as paranoid. Me and my former friend. I think I called him S, the one I went and a got the lap-dance beside. Anyway, one day we were over at this really unattractive girls house and she told us if we wanted pot readily just visit this guy, I'll call So and So. So one day me and S went over there unannounced and asked if we could get any mushrooms. Yes it was mushrooms and not pot at that time. So and So said he didn't have any, but would it be possible if I could take him to the liquor store in the next county over, being that we lived in a dry one. I agreed and as he piled in the back , S an I were parlayed with drunken mumblings of how he had been taking Valium all day. When we finally arrived S and I turned around to see a pasted out So and So. We both smiled at each other and knew we had met someone special. A complete stranger had just pasted out in the back of my car. I was beyond intrigued. We nudged him awake and as he stumbled out the car people started to laugh at his obvious over intoxication. He didn't even get the door shut. When we got back to his house he was kind enough to sell us some of the best pot we had ever had.

Later after we got to know each other. So and So and his wife said the only reason they decided to sell to us was because of S. S was a character. Homemade tattoos covered his arms. Long hair gave the impression of rebel. And over all appearance was destined to call for racial profiling.

So trips to So and So became daily visits. Soon as my three periods were over, over there I went. As my tolerance grew. So did my popularity. I was a regular feature at peer functions. And the best part was. Only I and S new of So and So. With boredom of the same high, which was becoming less and less longer. We started pestering So and So for acid. Finally giving up asking as the Senior year of high-school began its quick demise. I entered one Saturday afternoon and asked for the usual. He didn't reply and only smiled. I stood for a second wondering what he was doing. I remember his lips moving. He was teasing me for some reaction, I know now. Those lips were saying ACID!!! When I finally figured out what he was saying. I handed him my money and for the second time I was about to embark on a trip. I got two hits, one for me and the other for S. A couple joints as well to start the journey off quicker. When I got to S's house I decided it would be best to do a little teasing myself. That night, though vague, was one of the most irresponsible nights of my life. Which I don't see how I survived. See I thought it would be interesting to drive on acid. And so did my friend. The problem is we neglected to watch the weather channel that night.

The night had dampness in the air. And by the time our trip was before the level of peaking, we were driving in a storm I had never seen before in my life. Barely seeing past the hood of my car we drove to town, past State Troopers wise enough to pull off the road. Our ramblings took us to back roads, that were unfamiliar.

The next day as I stumbled in my home, I saw my father watching car racing and still the trip was still on. As I showered the sweat off my body, in the dark. Which is how I still like to shower. I turned to see the showerhead nozzle turn into a snake that scared me senseless. My problem the whole night was fighting it. When my shower finished. I went directly back to S's house. Which in turn lead us back to So and So's. S had gotten some money for the

impending graduation and instead of a few
hits, he got ten. Again that day we tripped. And
I found out later what bad trip means. As we
were driving down a road we had been on several times. My mind was bombarded with
every emotion one could have simultaneously
. Tears emerged in my eyes. My hand clutched
the wheel. S wisely instructed me to pull over
and relax. I don't think I have been the same
sense. I can't show a particular justification.
But that much acid in that small period of
time, must case someone to..................?

Did we stop? Of course not. We still had
Senior skip day to look forward to. So we headed
for the beach. As our classmates arrived and
stared at us and checked our obvious disposi-
tion. We sat in the car and watched events tran-
spire. Finally I was hit with an incredible
laughing fit. Everyone was staring at us. We had
been in that damn car for over an hour, mouths
agape. We got out of the car and proceeded to
get the folding chairs out of the trunk. There we
had a view of depravity at its most. One particular girl who never looked like much of a partier
was throwing-up in a near by barrel. Another
girl was running around frantic to get a hit off
every joint that was being pasted to and fro. And
still people looked at us with amusement. S and

I sat on our throne's like kings of some satanic drug festival. Girls exposing their selves. Alcohol flowing. A day long tribute to time changing mercilessly. Faces looked upon differently. You could almost feel the distantness. How those faces would possibly be seen again in ten years at some reunion. It was sad. Well that's what my vision of the events.

With much brain picking I have remembered one class of my Sophomore year. S an I had this English teacher, who was one of those types best made for Junior high. So armed with that powerful bias, we made her period a living hell.

The class was on the second floor of the school. On this particular day the windows were open and painting was being done outside. The paint fumes were lingering in at an alarming rate. We didn't dare close the windows because of the heat, however. People started centralizing on one side. Quickly the desks filled up. I had a wonderful idea and S followed suit. We generously gave our seats away and went to the most dangerous point. After some deep inhales we started to get good and buzzed. The teacher knew what we were doing. She did nothing about it however, I guess she hoped it would kill us. Now for some reason I got up to ask her a question. As I approached I saw her she was in conversation with another student. A sudden fit of laughter come upon. Within two feet I must have been of her, I started pointing and laughing. I turned back to S who shared my enthusiasm. I finally gave up trying to talk to her, or forgot the question I was going to ask. As I returned to my seat. Now in tears. S put up his hand to give an encouraging high-five. We swung our hands and missed badly. That in turn only made us laugh harder.

Another time in this class, some project was assigned. S , another slacker, and I chose to group together. I am positive it involved the direction of food preparation. While the others brought in elaborate meals. We brought in hotdogs and buns. Since everyone else had something written down to read their recipe off of. S quickly scribbled something on paper, laughing the whole time. I knew it was not going to be pretty. As he started his perverted explanation of how to get the hotdogs all hot and bothered. I watched the class. They didn't laugh, but every eye was wide, and every facial expression showed an excited blankness which I could not uncover the meaning. The teacher sat at the back of the room, you could almost see the steam of heat rising from her. When we finished, her only response went something like, 'can't you guys say anything without there being a sexual overtone?' S an I told her we had no idea what she was talking about and were rewarded with a F!

As for S. We remained friends. For the next few years. Everyday I would come to his house and we would get stoned. Pledging one day to get our act together. We eventually tried. We entered another counties college. But by that time I was a bad alcoholic. I could never stay there. I don't know why. Everyone was nice. S and I were friends with everyone. I past my first year. My second was a different story. I was a hermit. I would go to class, sweat pouring, feeling so self conscience. Feeling all eyes were on me. When all I wanted to be was a ghost. I felt predestined to be the watcher. The guy who writes about life, but never leads it. I guess I still am that way.

I don't recall what I said to S to hurt him so. I apologized once and we started talking. But he stopped calling. One day at a party I called him and he sounded less than enthused to hear my voice so I said, 'I will never bother you again.' And I haven't to this day. Sometimes I hate him and other times I miss him so much. He was a brother. We shared the same twisted sense of humor. The same ambitions of ruling the world.

I would like to think we will someday be friends again, but hold out little hope. We are both stubborn and for to long we have not known each other. Right now I wish him a good life. And would say, 'GOD bless you.' But tomorrow I will probably regret writing this. And even though my heart may change my words won't.

Another influential person in my life is and was Jim. I must explain now rather than go back and start the explanation where it should have began. As you probably have figured out. If for some chance I never get around to publishing my own memoirs. Because of lack of fame or death. I neglected to use real names for the sake of personal privacy and what not.

Anyway back to Jim. I knew Jim all through school. He had an oddness about him that pulled me in. Early years of school though, I liked him but hated him as well. He was just fucking mean. But with freshman year of high-school. We sat together in Science class. That is truly a class I shall not soon forget. It was so liberating from the evil of junior high. Mr. Cox, though menacing to look at, was a good teacher. With an easy sense of humor. It was a love/hate relationship from the start. He would say something and I would usually interpret it as him saying, 'TESTICLE,' and quickly call him on it.

Sometimes chastising him for such inappropriate language. One time as the class was talking Jim an I were setting there taking the waves of different speech in. Apparently we both had the same idea. We would take one groups conversation and implement it into someone else's. And so the first conversation went, best I recall, was about one girl trying to get away from some guy trying to grope her in a vehicle (not raping her). We turned to Mr. Cox's conversation to some student immediately and he said something along the lines of, 'i had to get out of my van.' Well that was enough for me to fall down in the floor laughing. Mr. Cox sprang into action. I happened to look up and see our teacher rush around his desk and go after Jim. Jim was quick and he jumped out of his seat, for obvious fear of the linebacker of a man. But he jumped to late and a kick to the ass sent Jim pummeling to the floor. Naturally scared I tried to get up. But I too was to late. And as his hands steadied themselves on my and Jim's desk, and the one behind us, he proceeded to go up and down with his knees on my chest. While doing that he screamed the words, 'I hate you,' over and over. Of course it didn't hurt. Thanks to his strong hands. But I sure got dirty.

Another time in class as he was teaching. I could tell he was excited. Jim an I hadn't acted up all day. But when he turned his attention to me an I smiled. I could see the hope of a peaceful day, drain from his once shiny exterior. I bided my time. And just when I thought I think of anything to do. I remembered that across from Jim sat a girl I'll call P. P was nice and fun to sexually harass. So when Mr. Cox's attention came back to me. I slipped my hand past Jim and slowly started to pull up P's short loose skirt. Keep in mind. The whole time I paid little attention to P's face and more so on his. It was an expression of, 'I can't believe this.' Eventually my hand was slapped and insults were directed toward me. The bell rang and I exited, with another memory under my belt.

Jim an I also had another Science teacher together, in our eleventh grade year. Her name was Mrs. Cravens. She was a certified genus. And also possessed ability to see things that were in peoples pockets and minds. That was sometime freaky. I remember one occasion as I sat outside the lunch room. She past, after about thirty feet I whispered her name. Not loud enough for the guy beside me to hear. She turned around and smiled and waved. But back to the class. The school kept putting me in advanced classes. The one she taught was chemistry. In that particular class they managed to put all the smart smart-asses. Upon noticing this I deemed myself leader. That first day was a blast. We got into a discussion about religion. Adam and Eve was the subject and the girls were bitching that Eve did-n't force Adam to eat the apple. I said, 'no but she said he could have some ass if he did.' Everyone was laughing already and with that they rolled. Jim got up at my behest and started jumping around like a rabbit. Suffice to say, soon the class was broken up. Just Jim an I remained.

Since I knew nothing about this class I just usually sat outside and wrote poetry. Two that I wrote outside that class have now been published, so the class wasn't a complete lose. Now Jim liked to make good grades. He's the type that irritates you by complaining to the teacher about it. This day she wasn't listening. Out of protest Jim set his paper ablaze. He got in a bit of trouble for that little shenanigan. Another time we were setting around and Jim asked if the chemistry lab had the necessary ingredients to make acid. Of course it didn't. Then not wanting to be left out of not getting a laugh as well. I asked if the chemistry lab had the ability to grow marijuana. I managed to pass her class though.

Thanks to her giving an A to everyone that last six weeks. It was her last year. I neglected to mention that Mr. Cox left the year after us as well. There was something about that whole class that made teachers quit. And we all took pride in the fact that the teachers must think if we are that bad, how awful could the next class be; who looked up to us.

Jim also was the first to introduce me to pot as well as alcohol. One time long ago. When he came back to town he picked me up and bought alcohol for us. I casually drank, well casually by my standards anyhow. He finally said, 'drink up. I am ahead of you.' I announced bluntly I was not drinking to throw-up. He got the message. Jim doesn't do anything anymore. He does drink on occasion. He asked for my forgiveness that night of all the peer-pressure he threw at me. It wasn't his fault, well partly, but I was pre-disposed to it. And handing problems off to others is not what I like to do. I am strong enough to ask for help and willingly except it. But I am no coward to responsibility.

Another friend whom I stay close to is Josh. Josh was probably the best influence among my friends. Hardly ever drank and to my knowledge only did that after his twenty-first birthday. And never judged others who did. His home was like

a home away from home. And I am sure he
would say vice-versa. We'd shoot hoops all
night. Watch movies, eat pizza, play video
games; all manor of such. I used to look forward
to the weekends away from the hell that was jun-
ior-high. And his older brothers were great as
well. Big guys no one messed with. And they
saved my ass more times than I can count. Josh
also showed me my fear of diving was right on.
He lived near an old creek. And one summer day
we went out there for a swim. There was two
places to dive. One a running leap off an
embankment, about ten feet up. Another was a
two by four another five feet, extra, off the
embankment. though I never tried the later. I
did try the embankment. As they were giving me
instructions on how to jump and position
myself properly for landing, I just took off. I ran
and leaped. And did a belly flop. Instead of
going into the water feet first. My next attempt
my strides were to far apart. And instead of
jumping I fell. If I had fallen to the right just a
few inches I would probably be dead, given that
there was a very large and sharp rock. But, luckily I just hurt my ankle. Up the road there was a
girl of Indian decent that desperately wanted to
go out with me. And at times wish she had been

my first lay. But alas, I again thought there would be someone better down the road.

Life after the periods I have talked about has been dull. Because of my drug use I have fallen far behind. And presently I am only twenty-three. Repeated behavior of watching movies over an over, drunk; searching for some sign. A sign that will never come. That's the alcoholic way though. Repeated unnatural behavior hoping for a different outcome. If by chance this is one day published, I want children to know. I didn't tell you these things to glamorize the world of drugs. Sure I had fun....THEN. Now I look at all those times and there's almost a post traumatic feel. I could have killed someone. Let alone myself. I hardly have bad dreams but when I do its of being arrested for another D.U.I.

My first arrest for D.U.I. came after being cooped up at home for nearly a month with no means of inebriation. I went out with some friends and drove into a ditch. Cops were called and I was arrested. I was so mad at myself. My face turned into rage at how I had screwed up. I must have looked like I was about to cry. But a familiar calmness hit me. I knew it wasn't the end of the world. I entered out-patient detoxification and told them what they wanted to hear.

But I didn't get better. I was still so young an invulnerable. When I got my license back, it didn't take long for my same reckless habits to take top priority again.

I remember vividly one time I almost died because of that old liquid courage. I was with some friends and as chance managed. I met a cousin I had never met before. We decided after much drink to drive to this isolated tower. They called it the fire tower, it was something so dangerous that that could be its only purpose. It went I am guessing well over a hundred feet in the air. Steps led up like any building. Except in the middle instead of a walkway there was a narrow beam of metal, no more than three inches wide that you had to step on to get to the other set of stairs. Keeping in mind that this was well into the pitch black darkness and that I was afraid of heights. We managed to get to the top. But just as quickly wanted to make our way back down. Halfway down, in a quick sprint, my foot misjudged where the beam of metal was. Luckily I was hanging on the handrail for support. My body just sank. Everyone froze. They were all in a panic but me. As I laid across that beam, looking down. A calmness hit me. I told them to grab my feet and pull back. They did and we managed to get down safely. Even writing this makes my heart patter wildly.

My second D.U.I. came after my first semester of college. I was less than a mile from home driving to fast and my car skidded out of control and hit an embankment. I was arrested and again went to counseling where I continue to stay. I managed to write my first book, SNOW WHITE HYPOCRISY. And things have improved. Maturity has come. But everyday I thank GOD or whatever spirit that I didn't kill someone. But I am CLEP testing now and will, hopefully, reenter a college soon. I sometimes want to kick myself for starting after high-school. But that only further hinders my progress.

September 11, was a day that the world stopped. Like that beautiful Alan Jackson song. I remember that day. Actually it started with that early morning. I remember having bad dreams that night. Like I have said I usually have night-mares about being caught for drinking and driv-ing but outside of that, I never have them. I remember with each dream I would wake up, with my torso springing up. Which was new too. The only dream I remember was of being in a building with rubble all around. Children's toys, confetti, a small group of people just standing around watching me. It wasn't a bad dream. It was rather peaceful, so I was shocked that I had sprung up yet again. By this time it was early morning. I decided, 'enough sleep.' So I got up and urged my parents to take me to town so I could buy a new C.D. player. As i waited for my mother to get ready I was watching the TODAY show. Matt was interviewing some fellow about a book he had just finished about Howard Hughes. I was always interested in interesting people so I watched. Then it happened. I was saddened, but figured it was a freak accident, like many did.

In the car I flipped through the channels and found that yet another plane had hit the other tower. At this I became worried. Something wasn't right. We drove past the discount store to the movie place I so seldom hung out at. I talked with the proprietor and rented the movie BLOW. My stomach was to much in shambles to worry about some trivial stereo. On the way home my mother's eyes filled with tears as the announcement of yet another plane crashing. This time into the Pentagon. I watched television all night and got drunk for the last time. The next day in between watching Brokaw and Jennings I found that our local station, as well as many others, as started a relief fund; in association with the Red Cross. At first hearing about it I called in. I was hesitate at first to send much, because of my dwindling bank account but conceded and gave one hundred dollars. I come close to chastising the man for his happiness to be getting what I would call a larger amount than most had given. But I decided best not to as I figured it was a renewed pride on his part to see a Country once so in conflict with itself now coming together. And by GOD did we. As I watched the continuing coverage I felt relief for the great leaders we had. President Bush was the man among men. When tears showed in his eyes from cameras watching him on the phone. To getting up in front a crowd and telling this great Nation and this World that a reckoning was coming, 'at our hour of choosing.' The cheers for Firepersons and Police Officers who risked life and limb. Who's comrades had fallen. You could almost see Grandfather's with Grandson's standing on their lawn putting up flags, as strangers past in cars, tears welling in their eyes. Norman Rockwell images you past every day. People who's faces looked at you differently. It was of a brotherhood and sisterhood. At no time had this great generation come across a struggle so paramount. And rise we did.

Truly the World stopped. The other Countries that so quickly erupted at any mistake we made, showed fear. Countries we wouldn't have expected offered their help as we always have. With food dropping we fed the people of Afghanistan. With our victory over city after city, town after town, we freed an oppressed people. The News cameras' showed faces of women for the first time. People celebrated by doing the simple act of shaving. At present the War on Terrorism is far from over. But I have absolute faith in President Bush and his genius Cabinet choosing. We stand by our leader. In times of crisis we always have. And though I have Native American blood in me that's red. It also contains white and blue.

I guess, though like with other things, should have brought up sooner. I will talk of my parents. Well like that bitch at the baby-sitter's said, their old. For standards of that time. My Mother not really but my father is. There is a huge generation gap between us. I heard he liked to drink allot. And one of his hobbies, in youth, was to drive fast and outrun the law. Tickets were issued at his place of employment by Officers who cared little for my fathers shit eating grin.

They never formally finished much of school but are avid readers. My Dad especially. Sunday morning church services for me eventually became watching This Week. And every night it was a fight to watch television because the only thing for him was public T.V.

My mother always worked. She was laid off from a Factory, as all employee's were, just a few years before she could retire. That was a burden because she lost her health insurance and had to spend most of her paycheck on prescription medication.

I don't remember traveling much I guess as they got older they didn't want to leave the house. We occasionally visit an aunt in Indiana. I had four Uncles on my father's side. And they all were mentally incompetent in some manor. I don't mind though. I have heard studies about people with mental retardation in their families also have a higher chance of genus. Which could very well be the case because at twenty-one I finished my first book. And I have a cousin who was a college professor.

In the later years all I remember is my family yelling. It was fun for them, I think.

To get completely off track again I will tell you more of my high-school experience. This revolves around the last day of my Sophomore year. Now most people would bring white t-shirts for everyone to sign. I thought this was to over done. So taking off the novelty bikini briefs I wore the day before. I became an original. I had Q sign and D. D by the way asked if they had ever been wore. Of course I lied. It was surprising that so many women willingly wrote on my underwear. The only one who didn't was a stuck up cousin in law. She was gorgeous though, I hate to admit my hand and I have role play acted.

I just remembered another story about Scott. At the end of Junior year. I didn't have a date for the prom. Scott stepped into action. He quickly secured me one. It was his dates friend. She was hot. Very top heavy. Though I got the sense that she didn't care much for me initially. I called her up one Saturday night and told her it would be wise to go out and at least get a feel of each other. A blind date at Prom didn't sound right. So we went out. I took her to a movie. I paid her way. Even though she didn't want me to. And soon as it was over. Still in the light of day, I took her home.

When prom came the Tux didn't fit. My sister had traded cars that day, unbeknownst to me. So I picked her up in a dirty car. We drove over to meet Scott and another guy. We went to a fancy restaurant out of town. On the drive my date started flirting with a group of guys in a truck.

Which sparked heated words. The meal was expensive and on the drive back we stopped at the local bootlegger and stockpiled up. Finally on the way to prom. We both came to agreement. We didn't want to go. She said there was a party. I knew this was bad from the beginning. A group of guys and a girl, who had already started to get hammered. We got there and she started talking to all these horny men. Luckily her brother-in-law was there and took over where I couldn't. The mother of the guy who threw the party was there and said she wasn't going to let me drive her home in the state I was in. But she gladly let me go. That, by the way, was the first time I drove drunk; sadly not the last. The only memory I have of her is a, what do you call those things, you take off their leg? I made no effort to go to Senior prom.

Another favorite teacher was Coach Gumm. He was like a big kid. I would sometimes go on fieldtrips with the team and videotape it. On one occasion out of town. I got diarrhea real bad. We pulled over at a rest stop and I had the greatest shit of my life. Coming out the whole bus was in an uproar to see me chug a bottle of Pepto. When we arrived we secured our rooms at a hotel. There were two girls along. And they quickly came to our rooms. D and F, I'll call them. I took a shower first and when I got out. I saw the girls on one bed and four guys on the other. I called them gay and hoped in bed between and was fully prepared to have an inter-racial threesome. But that damn coach, he had to put them in separate rooms. He also put bells on our door and theirs.

Now F was a red head. Which is funny I have had weird luck with red heads all my life. Two of them hated me beyond explanation, one I walked down the isle with at my sisters wedding, one I lost my virginity to, and two more wanted to date me. Put in F and three wanted to date me. The other D, she was African-American. And I wanted her bad. She asked me out one time Sophomore year. When I replied, 'can we do it.' She abruptly walked off. Looking back on it now I hate myself. There were so many nights when we would pull in and everyone would leave. Except me and her, left to wait for our parents. We could have made some beautiful and unbe-lievable memories in Coach's office. Or on the basketball court. Or in the teachers lounge. You get the point. GOD must hate me or love me. I counted over fifty women I could have been with sexually and the true amount I could count on one or two hands. Well that's the reason he must love me. The reason he must hate me is, "GOD hates a coward."

Did I ever tell you how my love affair for strippers began? I didn't think so. I was about sixteen or so. I won't say who took me, but lets say it would surprise you at his status in relation to me. One thing I must tell you while its on my mind about J. It's rumored she did private shows for a prominent Politician. But back to the first at a strip bar. Me and this person went in. They were willingly to let him in, but not me. I told them I had forgot my I.D. About five miles down the road a flash of brilliance hit me. I asked him if he had an old license. He said yes. I took out my student I.D. from school, it was about time it became useful for something. So we cut out my picture, peeled back his license and managed to tape my picture over his. We went back expecting to be turned away. But the guy ushered us in. I sat passive. For my first time in one of those clubs I was to say honestly, bored. I was excited to see a woman naked for the first time, actually several women naked. But it wasn't the erection charged, tongue dropping fiasco that I had envisioned. And that's it. We left. But away from such establishments I didn't. On my eighteenth birthday I went back, but had little fun. I decided it best to spend my money on drugs instead of on women with fake flattery.

Another time I went, was a few days after I got my first official paycheck. As un-luck would have it. The night I got paid my father had a heart attack. But days of worry proved false and he recovered never really having been in bad shape. So I picked up S and we went to a popular strip bar in the big city. I was at my prime then in looks. I was a security guard. I let my five o'clock shadow grow out and sported Tom Cruises' hair. When we went in, either all eyes were on me; and my stunning beauty. Or S and his out of this world look. We sat at a table away from the masses and within seconds a blue eyed beauty showed up. I won't go into details about what happened, but I will say I was bitten. When I got back to the table. The announcer announced that there were dollar lap-dances. They all came to me first. They formed a line that easily went twenty girls back. I was the man. Though in the back of my head I worried about my father. We left penny-less and somehow made it home on half a tank of gas.

Another friend I have yet to mention is Cory. We met when I was on summer vacation from the hell that was middle school. He and I were babysat by a cousin of mine. But we rarely stayed with her, for Cory's Grandparents lived in the house next door and were always at work. We would sneak into his Grandfathers room and devour the pictures in his Playboys. I saw Madonna naked! We often stayed the night at each others houses. I liked staying at his because he lived next to D. Though I never saw her it was a comfort being so close. The old saying haunted my mind those nights trying to sleep. Maybe she's looking at the same moon I am and if not at least she's a stones throw away. Cory got in trouble one night when his friends snuck out to get a glance in her bedroom window. Where they found her naked, lucky bastards. He wasn't involved and was quickly absolved of wrong doing.

Cory an I became so close, his parents took me on vacation with them. It was a two bed, side by side, room. Cory an I on one bed, his parents on the other. We watched T.V. for awhile and Cory and his mother fell asleep. His dad an I were watching a movie and when breasts were shown. I instinctively nudged Cory. I realized my blunder when I looked over and saw his dad with a wide grin. She said softly, 'about time to go to bed, don't you think?' I agreed, not wanting any further embarrassment.

I am running out of things to say, and now that the electricity is back on. I will give my parting thoughts. Maybe a bit of wisdom to boot. In my short lived life, through all my travels and heartbreak. I can't think of a reason why. To quote millions of people, 'you are given one life. Give it your best shot.' I don't know if the path I have chosen was my choosing or a higher-being. I would like to think a bit of both. When I drove drunk I was lucky not to have murdered anyone. That was my decision . What kept me and others alive, that had to have been some type of Divine hand.

Yet another friend I count as a blessing I will call Addiction. He came to our school for our Senior year. He was something new, straight from Los Angeles. He seemed like an interesting person. He was quiet in the beginning but eventually came around and started setting beside me. We started talking one day when he was playing with some item and was asked by a teacher if that was fun, he matter-of-factly exclaimed, 'if your on acid.' Addiction, S and I started hanging out. I remember one occasion Addiction came into first period bloody and limping. When we finally got around to asking what happened. He said he was hit by a car on the way to school. Actually it was a hit and run.

Another time he stumbled in class early. He asked if I wanted a beer, before I could say, 'NO.' He sat one on my desk. No one seemed surprise. But naturally I was worried about the teacher arriving. One time I took him home and was introduced to his brother. That was the first time I got high off cocaine. I mean high enough that I could recognize it. I shouldn't have driven that day either, but I did. Addiction saved my ass one night, and I will always be thankful for that. A friend I'll call T, actually he is no friend. He is an asshole who I wouldn't care to see dead. Anyway T had found out I about got into it with some guy. He told me to come to a local restaurant. I didn't ask why, I just followed. The guy was there and he was mad. From a distance we made a peace. When I turned back to T I saw him there. Blank faced. He quickly left though when he saw the seven inch, shiny blade in Addictions hands. So thanks again Addiction. And as for you T, bad things follow bad people. And I wish you all the pain in the world.

When I think about my friends a smile always comes to my face. I enjoyed writing this jumbled mess, and with time permitting continue off and on as new memories come. We see each other still but as we have matured so has come responsibility. Most of them all have significant others who come first, and I understand. I would blow them off too, if I were so engaged. A hundred million laughs long forgotten in my portal of mind and time. Obstacles overcome, victory's shared, enemies thwarted. Reading these words is sad. It almost makes me sound like I will die soon. And maybe I will. But I am consoled in the fact that I had a good life. I had my family, who were my best friends. Always there to get me out of a jam. Lend an ear, help me to attain the happiness that a rural upbringing did not offer them. Hopefully the cycle of life will be the same for me. Hopefully something wonderful will happen so I can give my children the way to achieve more than I have. My friends will always be a part of my life, no matter how far away. In life and death they will remain a part of this old soul. As I will be in theirs. And that family that is friendship will be inbred into our generations to come.

The love interests in my life will come and go. But if a young person should ever come upon reading this, and needs advice on how to overcome a heartache. I won't be so patronizing as to say, there are other fish in the sea. I will say, leave your pity behind for one day. Just one, and go out. Look around. If you let it go for just that one day, you'll find that old lust again. You'll make eye contact with someone, and who knows? As for me. I am content in that fact, through years of wisdom and heartbreak. I will look up at the moon now, listening to Ozzy's 'Dreamer.' And maybe she will be looking too. If not now then maybe 'someday.'

0-595-22687-6

Made in the USA
Las Vegas, NV
17 March 2022

45857413R00073